Total-E-Bound Publishing books by Isabelle Drake:

Invitations:
Now or Never
Dare Me

I0533682

Play for Keeps
Rock and Roll Fantasy

The Fox

A Clandestine Classic

D.H. LAWRENCE and ISABELLE DRAKE

The Fox
ISBN # 978-1-78184-595-0
©Copyright Isabelle Drake 2013
Cover Art by Posh Gosh ©Copyright June 2013
Interior text design by Claire Siemaszkiewicz
Total-E-Bound Publishing

The Fox

Dedication

For the faculty of the English Language and Literature Department at The University of Michigan, for the encouragement and support I received as an undergraduate.

Chapter One

The two girls were usually known by their surnames, Banford and March. They had taken the farm together, intending to work it all by themselves — that is, they were going to rear chickens, make a living by poultry, and add to this by keeping a cow, and raising one or two young beasts. Unfortunately, things did not turn out well.

Banford was a small, thin, delicate thing with spectacles. She, however, was the principal investor, for March had little or no money. Banford's father, who was a tradesman in Islington, gave his daughter the start, for her health's sake, and because he loved her, and because it did not look as if she would marry. March was more robust. She had learned carpentry and joinery at the evening classes in Islington. She would be the man about the place. They had, moreover, Banford's old grandfather living with them at the start. He had been a farmer. But unfortunately the old man died after he had been at Bailey Farm for a year. Then the two girls were left alone.

They were neither of them young—that is, they were near thirty. But they certainly were not old. They set out quite gallantly with their enterprise. They had numbers of chickens, black Leghorns and white Leghorns, Plymouths and Wyandottes, also some ducks, also two heifers in the fields. One heifer, unfortunately, refused absolutely to stay in the Bailey Farm closes. No matter how March made up the fences, the heifer was out, wild in the woods, or trespassing on the neighbouring pasture, and March and Banford were away, flying after her, with more haste than success. So this heifer they sold in despair. Then, just before the other beast was expecting her first calf, the old man died, and the girls, afraid of the coming event, sold her in a panic, and limited their attentions to fowls and ducks.

In spite of a little chagrin, it was a relief to have no more cattle on hand. Life was not made merely to be slaved away. Both girls agreed in this. The fowls were quite enough trouble. March had set up her carpenter's bench at the end of the open shed. Here she worked, making coops and doors and other appurtenances. By the end of her days spent there she was often a frightful mess, her hands torn from handling boards and her face dotted with sawdust. Banford didn't mind her friend's unusual appearance at all. Indeed, sometimes she would tease March. Those early days were filled with as much laughter as work.

The fowls, which gave the two women nothing to laugh about, were housed in the bigger building that had served as barn and cow-shed in old days. They had a beautiful home, and should have been perfectly content. Indeed, they looked well enough. But the girls were disgusted at their tendency to strange illnesses, at their exacting way of life and at their refusal, obstinate refusal to lay eggs.

March did most of the outdoor work. When she was out and about, in her puttees and breeches, her belted coat and her loose cap, she looked almost like some graceful, loose-balanced young man, for her shoulders were straight, and her movements easy and confident, even tinged with a little indifference or irony. But her face was not a man's face, ever. The wisps of her crisp dark hair blew about her as she stooped, her eyes were big and wide and dark, when she looked up again, strange, startled, shy and sardonic at once. Her mouth, too, was almost pinched as if in pain and irony. There was something odd and unexplained about her. She would stand balanced on one hip, looking at the fowls pattering about in the obnoxious fine mud of the sloping yard, and calling to her favourite white hen, which came in answer to her name. But there was an almost satirical flicker in March's big, dark eyes as she looked at her three-toed flock pottering about under her gaze, and the same slight dangerous satire in her voice as she spoke to the favoured Patty, who pecked at March's boot by way of friendly demonstration.

Fowls did not flourish at Bailey Farm, in spite of all that March did for them. When she provided hot food for them in the morning, according to rule, she noticed that it made them heavy and dozy for hours. She expected to see them lean against the pillars of the shed in their languid processes of digestion. And she knew quite well that they ought to be busily scratching and foraging about, if they were to come to any good. So she decided to give them their hot food at night, and let them sleep on it. Which she did. But it made no difference.

War conditions, again, were very unfavourable to poultry-keeping. Food was scarce and bad. And when the Daylight Saving Bill was passed, the fowls obstinately refused to go to bed as usual, about nine o'clock in the summer-time. That was late enough, indeed, for there was no peace till they were shut up and asleep. Now they cheerfully walked around, without so much as glancing at the barn, until ten o'clock or later. Both Banford and March disbelieved in living for work alone. They wanted to read or take a cycle-ride in the evening, or perhaps March wished to paint curvilinear swans on porcelain, with green background, or else make a marvellous fire-screen by processes of elaborate cabinet work. For she was a creature of odd whims and unsatisfied tendencies. But from all these things she was prevented by the stupid fowls.

One evil there was greater than any other. Bailey Farm was a little homestead, with ancient wooden barn and low-gabled farmhouse, lying just one field removed from the edge of the wood. Since the war the fox was a demon. He carried off the hens under the very noses of March and Banford. Banford would start and stare through her big spectacles with all her eyes, as another squawk and flutter took place at her heels. Too late! Another white Leghorn gone. It was disheartening.

They did what they could to remedy it. When it became permitted to shoot foxes, they stood sentinel with their guns, the two of them, at the favoured hours. But it was no good. The fox was too quick for them. So another year passed and another, and they were living on their losses, as Banford said. They let their farmhouse one summer, and retired to live in a railway-carriage that was deposited as a sort of outhouse in a corner of the field. This amused them, and helped their finances. None the less, things looked dark.

Although they were usually the best of friends, because Banford, though nervous and delicate, was a warm, generous soul, and March, though so odd and absent in herself, had a strange magnanimity, yet, in the long solitude, they were apt to become a little irritable with one another, tired of one another. March had four-fifths of the work to do, and though she did not mind, there seemed no relief, and it made her eyes flash curiously sometimes. Then Banford, feeling more nerve-worn than ever, would become despondent, and March would speak sharply to her. They seemed to be losing ground somehow, losing hope as the months went by. There alone in the fields by the wood, with the wide country stretching hollow and dim to the round hills of the White Horse, in the far distance, they seemed to have to live too much off themselves. There was nothing to keep them up—and no hope.

The fox really exasperated them both. As soon as they had let the fowls out, in the early summer mornings, they had to take their guns and keep guard, then again as soon as evening began to mellow, they must go once more. And he was so sly. He slid along in the deep grass. He was difficult as a serpent to see. And he seemed to circumvent the girls deliberately. Once or twice March had caught sight of the white tip of his brush, or the ruddy shadow of him in the deep grass, and she had let fire at him. But he made no account of this.

One evening March was standing with her back to the sunset, her gun under her arm, her hair pushed under her cap. She was half watching, half musing. It was her constant state. Her eyes were keen and observant, but her inner mind took no notice of what she saw. She was always lapsing into this odd, rapt state, her mouth rather screwed up. It was a question whether she was there, actually consciously present, or not.

The trees on the wood-edge were a darkish, brownish green in the full light—for it was the end of August. Beyond, the naked, copper-like shafts and limbs of the pine trees shone in the air. Nearer the rough grass, with its long, brownish stalks all agleam, was full of light. The fowls were round about—the ducks were still swimming on the pond under the pine trees. March looked at it all, saw it all and did not see it. She heard Banford speaking to the fowls in the distance—and she did not hear. What was she thinking about? Heaven knows. Her consciousness was, as it were, held back.

She lowered her eyes, and suddenly saw the fox. He was looking up at her. Her chin was pressed down, and his eyes were looking up. They met her eyes. And he knew her. She was spellbound—she knew he knew her. So he looked into her eyes, and her soul failed her. He knew her, he was not daunted.

She struggled, confusedly she came to herself, and saw him making off, with slow leaps over some fallen boughs, slow, impudent jumps. Then he glanced over his shoulder, and ran smoothly away. She saw his brush held smooth like a feather, she saw his white buttocks twinkle. And he was gone, softly, soft as the wind.

She put her gun to her shoulder, but even then pursed her mouth, knowing it was nonsense to pretend to fire. So she began to walk slowly after him, in the direction he had gone, slowly, pertinaciously.

She expected to find him. In her heart she was determined to find him. What she would do when she saw him again she did not consider. But she was determined to find him. So she walked abstractedly about on the edge of the wood, with wide, vivid dark eyes, and a faint flush in her cheeks. She did not think. In strange mindlessness she walked hither and thither.

At last she became aware that Banford was calling her. She made an effort of attention, turned, and gave some sort of screaming call in answer. Then again she was striding off towards the homestead. The red sun was setting, the fowls were retiring towards their roost. She watched them, white creatures, black creatures, gathering to the barn. She watched them spellbound, without seeing them. But her automatic intelligence told her when it was time to shut the door.

She went indoors to supper, which Banford had set on the table. Banford chatted easily. March seemed to listen, in her distant, manly way. She answered a brief word now and then. But all the time she was as if spellbound. And as soon as supper was over, she rose again to go out, without saying why.

She took her gun again and went to look for the fox. For he had lifted his eyes upon her, and his knowing look seemed to have entered her brain. She did not so much think of him—she was possessed by him. She saw his dark, shrewd, unabashed eye looking into her, knowing her. She felt him invisibly master her spirit. She knew the way he lowered his chin as he looked up, she knew his muzzle, the golden brown, and the greyish white. And again she saw him glance over his shoulder at her, half inviting, half contemptuous and cunning. So she went, with her great startled eyes glowing, her gun under her arm, along the wood edge. Meanwhile the night fell, and a great moon rose above the pine trees. And again Banford was calling.

So she went indoors. She was silent and busy. She examined her gun, and cleaned it, musing abstractedly by the lamplight. Then she went out again, under the great moon, to see if everything was right. When she saw the dark crests of the pine trees against the blood-red sky, again her heart beat to the fox, the fox. She wanted to follow him, with her gun.

It was some days before she mentioned the affair to Banford. Then suddenly one evening she said, "The fox was right at my feet on Saturday night."

"Where?" said Banford, her eyes opening behind her spectacles.

"When I stood just above the pond."

"Did you fire?" cried Banford.

"No, I didn't."

"Why not?"

"Why, I was too much surprised, I suppose."

It was the same old, slow, laconic way of speech March always had. Banford stared at her friend for a few moments.

"You saw him?" she cried.

"Oh yes! He was looking up at me, cool as anything."

"I tell you," cried Banford, "the cheek! They're not afraid of us, Nellie."

"Oh, no," said March.

"Pity you didn't get a shot at him," said Banford.

"Isn't it a pity! I've been looking for him ever since. But I don't suppose he'll come so near again."

"I don't suppose he will," said Banford.

And she proceeded to forget about it, except that she was more indignant than ever at the impudence of the beggar. March also was not conscious that she thought of the fox. But whenever she fell into her half-musing, when she was half rapt and half intelligently aware of what passed under her vision, then it was the fox which somehow dominated her unconsciousness, possessed the blank half of her musing. And so it was for weeks, and months. No matter whether she had been climbing the trees for the apples, or beating down the last of the damsons, or whether she had been digging out the ditch from the duck-pond, or clearing out the barn. When she had finished, or when she straightened herself, and pushed the wisps of her hair away again from her forehead, and pursed up her mouth again in an odd, screwed fashion, much too old for her years, there was sure to come over her mind the old spell of the fox, as it came when he was looking at her. It was as if she could smell him at these times. And it always recurred, at unexpected moments, just as she was going to sleep at night, or just as she was pouring the water into the teapot to make tea — it was the fox, it came over her like a spell.

So the months passed. She still looked for him unconsciously when she went towards the wood. He had become a settled effect in her spirit, a state permanently established, not continuous, but always recurring. She did not know what she felt or thought — only the state came over her, as when he looked at her.

The months passed, the dark evenings came, heavy, dark November, when March went about in high boots, ankle deep in mud, when the night began to fall at four o'clock, and the day never properly dawned. Both girls dreaded these times. They dreaded the almost continuous darkness that enveloped them on their desolate little farm near the wood. Banford was physically afraid. She was afraid of tramps, afraid lest someone should come prowling around. March was not so much afraid as uncomfortable, and disturbed. She felt discomfort and gloom in all her physique.

Usually the two girls had tea in the sitting room. March lighted a fire at dusk, and put on the wood she had chopped and sawed during the day. Then the long evening was in front, dark, sodden, black outside, lonely and rather oppressive inside, a little dismal. March was content not to talk, but Banford could not keep still. Merely listening to the wind in the pines outside or the drip of water, was too much for her.

One evening the girls had washed up the teacups in the kitchen, and March had put on her house-shoes, and taken up a roll of crochet-work, which she worked at slowly from time to time. So she lapsed into silence. Banford stared at the red fire, which, being of wood, needed constant attention. She was afraid to begin to read too early, because her eyes would not bear any strain. So she sat staring at the fire, listening to the distant sounds, sound of cattle lowing, of a dull, heavy moist wind, of the rattle of the evening train on the little railway not far off. She was almost fascinated by the red glow of the fire.

Suddenly both girls started, and lifted their heads. They heard a footstep—distinctly a solid, heavy footstep. Banford recoiled in fear. March stood listening. Then rapidly she approached the door that led into the kitchen. At the same time they heard the footsteps approach the back door. They waited a second. The back door opened softly. Banford gave a loud cry. A man's voice said softly, "Hello!"

March recoiled, and took a gun from a corner.

"What do you want?" she cried, in a sharp voice.

Again the soft, softly-vibrating man's voice said, "Hello! What's wrong?"

"I shall shoot!" cried March. "What do you want?"

"Why, what's wrong? What's wrong?" came the soft, wondering, rather scared voice, and a young soldier, with his heavy kit on his back, advanced into the dim light. He stood before the two women, a dark stranger.

"Why," he said, his voice, masculine and unfamiliar, giving each of them a shiver along their spine, "who lives here then?"

"We live here," said March. "What do you want?"

"Oh!" came the long, melodious, wonder-note from the young soldier. "Doesn't William Grenfel live here then?"

"No—you know he doesn't."

"Do I? Do I? I don't, you see. He did *live* here, because he was my grandfather, and I lived here myself five years ago. What's become of him then?"

The young man—or youth, for he would not be more than twenty—now advanced and stood in the inner doorway. March, under the influence of his strange, soft, modulated voice, stared at him spellbound. He had a ruddy, roundish face, with fairish hair, rather long, flattened to his forehead with sweat. His eyes were blue, and very bright and sharp. On his cheeks, on the fresh ruddy skin were fine, fair hairs, like a down, but sharper. It gave him a slightly glistening look. Having his heavy sack on his shoulders, he stooped, thrusting his head forward. His hat was loose in one rough, strong hand. He stared brightly, very keenly from girl to girl, particularly at March, who stood pale, with great dilated eyes, in her belted coat and puttees, her hair knotted in a big crisp knot behind. She still had the gun in her hand. Behind her, Banford, clinging to the sofa-arm, was shrinking away, with half-averted head.

"I thought my grandfather still lived here? I wonder if he's dead."

The three of them stood in silence, the young man's gaze moving from March to Banford then back to March, while the two women, each with her own concerns, looked the youth over. They took in all the details of him again.

"We've been here for three years," said Banford, who was beginning to recover her wits, seeing something boyish in the round head with its rather long, sweaty hair.

"Three years! You don't say so! And you don't know who was here before you?"

"I know it was an old man, who lived by himself."

"Ay! Yes, that's him. And what became of him then?"

"He died. I know he died."

"Ay! He's dead then."

The youth stared at them without changing colour or expression. If he had any expression, besides a slight baffled look of wonder, it was one of sharp curiosity concerning the two girls—sharp, impersonal curiosity, the curiosity of that round young head.

But to March he was the fox. Whether it was the thrusting forward of his head, or the glisten of fine whitish hairs on the ruddy cheek-bones, or the bright, keen eyes, that can never be said—but the boy was to her the fox, and she could not see him otherwise. Deep in her bones she knew the truth of it as she knew his hunting would be relentless.

"How is it you didn't know if your grandfather was alive or dead?" asked Banford, recovering her natural sharpness.

"Ay, that's it," replied the softly-breathing youth. He moved his hat to his other hand, again drawing the rapt gazes of the women. "You see, I joined up in Canada, and I hadn't heard for three or four years. I ran away to Canada."

"And now have you just come from France?"

"Well—from Salonika really." His fingers flicked across the hat. Each of his movements was another opportunity for the women to watch and study him. Especially March, who appreciated how crafty a fox must be.

There was a pause, nobody knowing quite what to say.

"So you've nowhere to go now?" said Banford rather lamely.

March stiffened at Banford's words. Where the youth had to go was not their concern. But then, he was on their doorstep. Perhaps they had to do something for him.

"Oh, I know some people in the village. Anyhow, I can go to the Swan."

"You came on the train, I suppose. Would you like to sit down a bit?"

"Well—I don't mind."

He gave an odd little groan as he swung off his kit. Banford looked at March.

"Put the gun down," she said. "We'll make a cup of tea."

"Ay," said the youth. "We've seen enough of rifles."

He sat down rather tired on the sofa, leaning forward. His lean, angular body was mannish and very out of place in the home of these two women who rarely—if ever—entertained male visitors.

March recovered her presence of mind, and went into the kitchen. There she heard the soft young voice musing, "Well, to think I should come back and find it like this!" He did not seem sad, not at all—only rather interestedly surprised.

"And what a difference in the place, eh?" he continued, looking round the room.

"You see a difference, do you?" said Banford.

"Yes—don't I!"

His eyes were unnaturally clear and bright, though it was the brightness of abundant health.

March was busy in the kitchen preparing another meal. It was about seven o'clock. All the time, while she was active, she was attending to the youth in the sitting room, not so much listening to what he said as feeling the soft run of his voice and the heavy weight of his presence. She primmed up her mouth tighter and tighter, puckering it as if it were sewed, in her effort to keep her will uppermost. Yet her large eyes dilated and glowed in spite of her. She lost herself. Rapidly and carelessly she prepared the meal, cutting large chunks of bread and margarine—for there was no butter. She racked her brain to think of something else to put on the tray—she had only bread, margarine and jam, and the larder was bare. Unable to conjure anything up, she went into the sitting room with her tray.

She did not want to be noticed. Above all, she did not want him to look at her. But when she came in, and was busy setting the table just behind him, he pulled himself up from his sprawling, and turned and looked over his shoulder. He saw her and she felt him. Impossibly, she felt him everywhere, as though he were touching her with his quick, busy hands, touching her with his nervous inquisitiveness. She became pale and wan. It was because of the odd response of her heart, forcing blood away from her skin and deep inside her body. She shivered from the effect.

The youth watched her as she bent over the table, looked at her slim, well-shapen legs, at the belted coat dropping around her thighs, showing him each curve of her hips. He looked at the knot of dark hair, and his curiosity, vivid and widely alert, was again arrested by her.

The lamp was shaded with a dark-green shade, so that the light was thrown downwards and the upper half of the room was dim. His face moved bright under the light, but March loomed shadowy in the distance. The two were sizing each other up, perhaps without knowing it, but that was the truth of the matter.

She turned round, but kept her eyes sideways, dropping and lifting her dark lashes in a movement she remembered from her own youth. Her mouth unpuckered as she said to Banford, "Will you pour out?"

Then to get away from him and the danger he had brought to their peaceful and quiet doorstep she went into the kitchen again. But leaving the room wasn't enough, the odd hot chill he'd created in their house followed her, chasing her.

"Have your tea where you are, will you?" said Banford to the youth. "Unless you'd rather come to the table."

March could hear her from the kitchen. She stayed breathless, awaiting the youth's reply and listening for the rasp of his deep voice and bracing for its effect upon her.

"Well," said he, "I'm nice and comfortable here, aren't I? I will have it here, if you don't mind."

"There's nothing but bread and jam," she said. And she put his plate on a stool by him. She was very happy now, waiting on him. For she loved company. And now she was no more afraid of him than if he were her own younger brother. He was such a boy.

"Nellie," she called. "I've poured you a cup out."

March appeared in the doorway, took her cup, and sat down in a corner, as far from the light as possible. She was very sensitive in her knees. Having no skirts to cover them, and being forced to sit with them boldly exposed, she suffered. She shrank and shrank, trying not to be seen. And the youth sprawling low on the couch, glanced up at her, with long, steady, penetrating looks, till she was almost ready to disappear. Yet she held her cup balanced, she drank her tea, screwed up her mouth and held her head averted. Her desire to be invisible was so strong that it quite baffled the youth. He felt he could not see her distinctly as he had moments ago. She seemed like a shadow within the shadow. And ever his eyes came back to her, searching, unremitting, with unconscious fixed attention.

Meanwhile he was talking softly and smoothly to Banford, who loved nothing so much as gossip, and who was full of perky interest, like a bird. Also he ate largely and quickly and voraciously, so that March had to cut more chunks of bread and margarine, for the roughness of which Banford apologised with soft, gentle words.

"Oh, well," said March, suddenly speaking, "if there's no butter to put on it, it's no good trying to make dainty pieces."

Again the youth watched her, and he laughed, with a sudden, quick laugh, showing his teeth and wrinkling his nose. March's heart quickened its pace, but she was growing accustomed to her response to him, and so she breathed more deeply to ease the discomfort of his stare.

"It isn't, is it," he answered in his soft, near voice.

It appeared he was Cornish by birth and upbringing. When he was twelve years old he had come to Bailey Farm with his grandfather, with whom he had never agreed very well. So he had run away to Canada, and worked far away in the West. Now he was here — and that was the end of it.

He was very curious about the girls, to find out exactly what they were doing. His questions were those of a farm youth — acute, practical, a little mocking. He was very much amused by their attitude to their losses, for they were amusing on the score of heifers and fowls.

"Oh, well," broke in March, "we don't believe in living for nothing but work."

"Don't you?" he answered. And again the quick young laugh came over his face. He kept his eyes steadily on the obscure woman in the corner.

"But what will you do when you've used up all your capital?" he said.

"Oh, I don't know," answered March laconically. "Hire ourselves out for land-workers, I suppose."

"Yes, but there won't be any demand for women land-workers now the war's over," said the youth.

"Oh, we'll see. We shall hold on a bit longer yet," said March, with a plangent, half-sad, half-ironical indifference.

"There wants a man about the place," said the youth softly.

Banford burst out laughing. For she herself saw the humour in their situation and knew that her laughter would be understood by the others. But the laughter was also a chance to let free some of the confusion she felt inside as she looked at the young man seated in what had been their very predictable and common home.

"Take care what you say," she interrupted. "We consider ourselves quite efficient."

"Oh," came March's slow plangent voice, "it isn't a case of efficiency, I'm afraid. If you're going to do farming you must be at it from morning till night, and you might as well be a beast yourself."

"Yes, that's it," said the youth. "You aren't willing to put yourselves into it."

"We aren't," said March, "and we know it." She said these words even though she herself had the rough hands and raw knees of one who did in fact put themselves into it.

"We want some of our time for ourselves," said Banford.

March looked at the other woman who, unlike herself, spoke honestly.

The youth threw himself back on the sofa, his face tight with laughter, and laughed silently but thoroughly. The calm scorn of the girls tickled him tremendously.

"Yes," he said, "but why did you begin then?"

"Oh," said March, "we had a better opinion of the nature of fowls then than we have now." And that was the truth and voicing it eased her.

"Of Nature altogether, I'm afraid," said Banford. "Don't talk to me about Nature."

Again the face of the youth tightened with delighted laughter.

"You haven't a very high opinion of fowls and cattle, have you?" he said.

"Oh no—quite a low one," said March, turning to move her knees from the light.

He laughed out. March watched his mouth, opening and closing, twisting, giving more expression to his face, for his blue eyes seemed to be in a constant state of curiosity. She looked at his hands, watched his long fingers grip the cup of tea.

"Neither fowls nor heifers," said Banford, "nor goats nor the weather."

The youth broke into a sharp yap of laughter, delighted. The girls began to laugh too, March turning aside her face and wrinkling her mouth in amusement.

"Oh, well," said Banford, "we don't mind, do we, Nellie?"

"No," said March, "we don't mind."

The youth was very pleased. He had eaten and drunk his fill. Banford began to question him. His name was Henry Grenfel—no, he was not called Harry, always Henry. He continued to answer with courteous simplicity, grave and charming. March, who was not included, cast long, slow glances at him from her recess, as he sat there on the sofa, his hands clasping his knees, his face under the lamp bright and alert, turned to Banford. She became almost peaceful at last. He was identified with the fox—and he was here in full presence. She need not go after him any more. There in the shadow of her corner she gave herself up to a warm, relaxed peace, almost like sleep, accepting the spell that was on her. But she wished to remain hidden. She was only fully at peace whilst he forgot her, talking to Banford. Hidden in the shadow of the corner, she need not any more be divided in herself, trying to keep up two planes of consciousness.

She could at last lapse into the odour and commanding strength of the fox.

For the youth, sitting before the fire in his uniform, sent a faint but distinct odour into the room, indefinable, but something like a wild creature. A scent that sank deep into the pores of the women in the room. Banford chatted on, ignited in her own way by the scent and the possibilities it represented. March no longer tried to reserve herself from it. She was still and soft in her corner like a passive creature in its cave. Her body was heated from her own blood, stirred by her heart, which had already become accustomed to responding to the young man. It was inevitable, she saw that now, that the fox would find her and she would be released, if only for a while, from the arduous hunt.

At last the talk dwindled. The youth relaxed his clasp of his knees, pulled himself together a little, and looked round. Again he became aware of the silent, half-invisible woman in the corner. She had been acutely aware of him the whole time and now that he had spotted her she was stirred and ready, although she wasn't quite certain what she was ready for, or even if she welcomed such readiness.

"Well," he said unwillingly, "I suppose I'd better be going, or they'll be in bed at the Swan."

"I'm afraid they're in bed, anyhow," said Banford, her voice still light and chatty, happy for another occasion to pass on news of others. "They've all got this influenza."

"Have they!" he exclaimed. And he pondered. March observed his mouth again moving as he considered the consequences and possibilities. "Well," he continued, "I shall find a place somewhere."

"I'd say you could stay here, only —" Banford began.

He turned and watched her, holding his head forward.

"What?" he asked.

"Oh, well," she said, "propriety, I suppose." She was rather confused.

"It wouldn't be improper, would it?" he said, gently surprised.

"Not as far as we're concerned," said Banford.

"And not as far as *I'm* concerned," he said, with grave naivete. "After all, it's my own home, in a way."

Banford smiled at this, her soft face glowing behind her spectacles.

"It's what the village will have to say," she said.

There was a moment's blank pause. Banford remained bright and at ease while March brewed with thick understanding. Foxes do not leave easily, once established. Why should they, she wondered, when they have all they need before them? And the helpless creatures whose lives they snatch at will, what is to become of them? They are powerless and so the fox will decide their fates.

"What do you say, Nellie?" asked Banford.

"I don't mind," said March, in her distinct tone. "The village doesn't matter to me, anyhow."

"No," said the youth, quick and soft. "Why should it? I mean, what should they say?"

"Oh, well," came March's plangent, laconic voice, "they'll easily find something to say. But it makes no difference what they say. We can look after ourselves."

"Of course you can," said the youth.

"Well then, stop if you like," said Banford. "The spare room is quite ready."

His face shone with pleasure.

"If you're quite sure it isn't troubling you too much," he said, with that soft courtesy which distinguished him.

"Oh, it's no trouble," they both said.

He looked, smiling with delight, from one to another.

"It's awfully nice not to have to turn out again, isn't it?" he said gratefully.

"I suppose it is," said Banford.

March disappeared to attend the room. Banford was as pleased and thoughtful as if she had her own young brother home from France. It gave her just the same kind of gratification to attend on him, to get out the bath for him, and everything. Her natural warmth and kindliness had now an outlet. And the youth luxuriated in her sisterly attention. But it puzzled him slightly to know that March was silently working for him too. She was so curiously silent and obliterated. It seemed to him he had not really seen her. She continued to elude him. He felt he should not know her if he met her in the road.

That night March dreamt vividly.

She dreamt she heard a singing outside, which she could not understand, a singing that roamed round the house, in the fields, and in the darkness. It moved her so that she felt she must weep.

She went out, and suddenly she knew it was the fox singing. He was very yellow and bright, like corn. She went nearer to him, but he ran away and ceased singing. He seemed near, and she wanted to touch him to feel that wild combination of roughness and beauty. She wanted him to know she was there, so she stretched out her hand, but suddenly he bit her wrist, and at the same instant, as she drew back, the fox, turning round to bound away, whisked his brush across her face, and it seemed his brush was on fire, for it seared and burned her mouth with a great pain.

The pain poured down from her mouth, through her breasts and deep into her centre. The sensation was quite fierce and relentless. It curled through her with slow stealth, seeping into her.

Deep in her sleep, she fought against it, but there was no escape. Eventually her body accepted the invasion and allowed it to sink deeper, even though the ongoing anguish caused her to twitch and turn, so much so that she woke Banford who was sleeping peacefully.

The other woman called out her name several times.

Finally she awoke with the pain of it, and lay trembling as if she were really seared.

In the morning, however, she only remembered it as a distant memory. She arose and was busy preparing the house and attending to the fowls. Banford flew into the village on her bicycle to try and buy food. She was a hospitable soul. But alas, in the year 1918 there was not much food to buy.

The youth came downstairs in his shirt-sleeves. He was young and fresh, but he walked with his head thrust forward, so that his shoulders seemed raised and rounded, as if he had a slight curvature of the spine. It must have been only a manner of bearing himself, for he was young and vigorous. The movements of his body were strong, confident and not complicated by thought or worry. He washed himself and went outside, whilst the women were preparing breakfast.

He saw everything, and examined everything. His curiosity was quick and insatiable. He compared the state of things with that which he remembered before, and cast over in his mind the effect of the changes. He watched the fowls and the ducks, to see their condition. He noticed the flight of wood-pigeons overhead—they were very numerous. He saw the few apples high up, which March had not been able to reach. He remarked that they had borrowed a draw-pump, presumably to empty the big soft-water cistern which was on the north side of the house.

"It's a funny, dilapidated old place," he said to the girls, as he sat at breakfast.

His eyes were wise and childish with thinking about things. He did not say much, but ate largely. March kept her face averted. She, too, in the early morning could not be aware of him, though something about the glint of his khaki reminded her of the brilliance of her dream-fox. And that pain, she remembered enough of it to wince each time he grabbed another hunk of bread or when he reached forward for his tea. Of course his gaze was upon her, ever inquisitive. His steady stare made her discomfort greater and she often turned to Banford, asking a question she wasn't truly interested in.

During the day the girls went about their business. In the morning he attended to the guns, shot a rabbit and a wild duck that was flying high towards the wood. That was a great addition to the empty larder. The girls felt that already he had earned his keep. He said nothing about leaving, however. In the afternoon he went to the village. He came back at teatime. He had the same alert, forward-reaching look on his roundish face. He hung his hat on a peg with a little swinging gesture. He was thinking about something.

"Well," he said to the girls, as he sat at table. "What am I going to do?"

"How do you mean—what are you going to do?" said Banford.

"Where am I going to find a place in the village to stay?" he said.

"I don't know," said Banford. "Where do you think of staying?"

"Well"—he hesitated—"at the Swan they've got this flu, and at the Plough and Harrow they've got the soldiers who are collecting the hay for the army. Besides, in the private houses, there's ten men and a corporal altogether billeted in the village, they tell me. I'm not sure where I could get a bed."

He left the matter to them. He was rather calm about it. March sat with her elbows on the table, her two hands supporting her chin, looking at him unconsciously. Suddenly he lifted his clouded blue eyes, and unthinking looked straight into March's eyes. The intensity of his gaze made her limbs immobile while her heart pumped wildly inside her chest. He was startled as well as she. He, too, recoiled a little but only with his body. His physical presence seemed to fill the entire room, blocking out everything and everyone—even the entire town. March felt the same sly, taunting, knowing spark leap out of his eyes, as he turned his head aside, and fall into her soul, as it had fallen from the dark eyes of the fox. She pursed her mouth as if in pain, as if asleep too.

"Well, I don't know," Banford was saying. She seemed reluctant, as if she were afraid of being imposed upon. She looked at March until March was finally able to look away from the young man. But, with her weak, troubled sight, Banford only saw the usual semi-abstraction on her friend's face. "Why don't you speak, Nellie?" she said.

But March was wide-eyed and silent, and the youth, as if fascinated, was watching her without moving his eyes.

"Go on—answer something," said Banford. And March turned her head slightly aside, as if coming to consciousness, or trying to come to consciousness.

"What do you expect me to say?" she asked automatically.

"Say what you think," said Banford.

"It's all the same to me," said March. She knew that the fox was sly and would have its way. There was not much reason to *think* where the fox was concerned. What was going to happen would simply happen. And she would respond one way or another.

And again there was silence. A pointed light seemed to be on the boy's eyes, penetrating like a needle.

"So it is to me," said Banford. "You can stop on here if you like."

A smile like a cunning little flame came over his face, suddenly and involuntarily. He dropped his head quickly to hide it, and remained with his head dropped, his face hidden. But March knew it was there, that smile that controlled her heart, making it circulate hot blood, preparing her body for whatever it was that the man wanted to take from her. Anything and everything. He would take and take until he had everything he wanted and she would be powerless to prevent it.

"You can stop on here if you like. You can please yourself, Henry," Banford concluded.

Still he did not reply, but remained with his head dropped. Then he lifted his face. It was bright with a curious light, as if exultant, and his eyes were strangely clear as he watched March. She turned her face aside, her mouth suffering as if wounded, and her consciousness dim.

Banford became a little puzzled. She watched the steady, pellucid gaze of the youth's eyes as he looked at March, with the invisible smile gleaming on his face. She did not know how he was smiling, for no feature moved. It seemed only in the gleam, almost the glitter of the fine hairs on his cheeks. Then he looked with quite a changed look at Banford.

"I'm sure," he said in his soft, courteous voice, "you're awfully good. You're too good. You don't want to be bothered with me, I'm sure."

"Cut a bit of bread, Nellie," said Banford uneasily, adding, "It's no bother, if you like to stay. It's like having my own brother here for a few days. He's a boy like you are."

"That's awfully kind of you," the lad repeated. "I should like to stay ever so much, if you're sure I'm not a trouble to you."

"No, of course you're no trouble. I tell you, it's a pleasure to have somebody in the house beside ourselves," said warm-hearted Banford.

"But Miss March?" he said in his soft voice, looking at her.

"Oh, it's quite all right as far as I'm concerned," said March vaguely. She might as well let it be all right, for she understood the fox as well as he understood her. The fox stayed wherever it was content and had all it needed.

His face beamed, and he almost rubbed his hands with pleasure.

"Well then," he said, "I should love it, if you'd let me pay my board and help with the work."

"You've no need to talk about board," said Banford.

One or two days went by, and the youth stayed on at the farm. Banford was quite charmed by him. He was so soft and courteous in speech, not wanting to say much himself, preferring to hear what she had to say, and to laugh in his quick, half-mocking way. He helped readily with the work—but not too much. He loved to be out alone with the gun in his hands, to watch, to see. For his sharp-eyed, impersonal curiosity was insatiable, and he was most free when he was quite alone, half-hidden, watching.

Particularly he watched March. She was a strange character to him. Her figure, like a graceful young man's, piqued him. Her dark eyes made something rise in his soul, with a curious elate excitement, when he looked into them—an excitement he was afraid to let be seen, it was so keen and secret. And her odd, shrewd speech made him laugh outright. He felt he must go further, he was inevitably impelled to go after this new prey. But he put away the thought of her and went off towards the wood's edge with the gun.

The dusk was falling as he came home, and with the dusk, a fine, late November rain. He saw the fire-light leaping in the window of the sitting room, a leaping light in the little cluster of the dark buildings. And he thought to himself it would be a good thing to have this place for his own. Then the thought entered him shrewdly. Why not marry March?

He stood still in the middle of the field for some moments, the dead rabbit hanging still in his hand, arrested by this thought. His mind waited in amazement—it seemed to calculate—and he smiled curiously to himself in acquiescence. Why not? Why not indeed? It was a good idea. What if it was rather ridiculous? What did it matter? What if she was older than he? It didn't matter. When he thought of her dark, startled, vulnerable eyes he smiled subtly to himself and thought of cold nights and the possibilities of the darkness. He was older than she, really. He was master of her and he would be sure she understood she did not have any control over him.

He scarcely admitted his intention even to himself. He kept it as a secret even from himself. It was all too uncertain as yet. He would have to see how things went. Yes, he would have to see how things went. If he wasn't careful, she would just simply mock at the idea. He knew, sly and subtle as he was, that if he went to her plainly and said, 'Miss March, I love you and want you to marry me,' her inevitable answer would be, 'Get out. I don't want any of that tomfoolery.' This was her attitude to men and their 'tomfoolery'. If he was not careful, she would turn round on him with her savage, sardonic ridicule, and dismiss him from the farm and from her own mind for ever.

He would have to go gently, carefully, slowly. He would have to catch her as you catch a deer or a woodcock when you go out shooting. It's no good walking out into the forest and saying to the deer, 'Please fall to my gun'. No, it is a slow, subtle battle. A battle where one is in control and the other only believes themselves to be in control.

When you really go out to get a deer, you gather yourself together, you coil yourself inside yourself, and you advance secretly, before dawn, into the mountains. The deer is already caught even though he does not know it. It is not so much what you do, when you go out hunting, as how you feel. You have to be subtle and cunning and absolutely fatally ready. It becomes like a fate. Your own fate overtakes and determines the fate of the deer you are hunting.

First of all, even before you come in sight of your quarry, there is a strange battle, like mesmerism. Your own soul, as a hunter, has gone out to fasten on the soul of the deer, even before you see any deer. And the soul of the deer fights to escape. Even before the deer has any wind of you, it is so. It is a subtle, profound battle of wills which takes place in the invisible. And it is a battle never finished till your bullet goes home. When you are really worked up to the true pitch, and you come at last into range, you don't then aim as you do when you are firing at a bottle. It is your own will which carries the bullet into the heart of your quarry. The bullet's flight home is a sheer projection of your own fate into the fate of the deer. It happens like a supreme wish, a supreme act of volition, not as a dodge of cleverness.

He was a huntsman in spirit, not a farmer, and not a soldier stuck in a regiment. And it was as a young hunter that he wanted to bring down March as his quarry, to make her his wife. So he gathered himself subtly together, seemed to withdraw into a kind of invisibility. He was not quite sure how he would go on. And March was suspicious as a hare. So he remained in appearance just the nice, odd stranger-youth, staying for a fortnight on the place.

He had been sawing logs for the fire in the afternoon and his entire body had been, at one point, covered in a fine sheen of perspiration. What remained now was the scent of his exertion and the lingering effects of the satisfaction that came across a man when he had done a hard job well.

Darkness came very early. It was still a cold, raw mist. It was getting almost too dark to see. A pile of short sawed logs lay beside the trestle. March came to carry them indoors, or into the shed, as he was busy sawing the last log. He was working in his shirt-sleeves, and did not notice her approach. She came unwillingly, as if shy. When she bent down he saw the firmness of her muscles and the easy way her strong arms moved the logs. She was a fine prey indeed and they both knew it. He saw her stooping to the bright-ended logs, and he stopped sawing, letting his probing gaze rake across her. A fire like lightning flew down his legs in the nerves and he was more aware of March than he ever had been. Everything about her called to him, her scent, her body, her essence. It was not enough to be near her. He needed to possess her. Indeed, master her.

"March?" he said in his quiet, young voice.

She looked up from the logs she was piling.

"Yes!" she said.

He looked down on her in the dusk. He could see her not too distinctly and he struggled to see what he could of her. If only she would stop shrinking away from him and expose herself to him as she ought to.

"I wanted to ask you something," he said, feeling that lightning fire burn in his limbs.

"Did you? What was it?" she said. Already the fright was in her voice. But she was too much mistress of herself. And it was that control, he realised, that he most wanted to take from her. She would weaken and give herself to him. He would see to it. As he felt that was what he wanted, he knew she must want it too.

"Why" — his voice seemed to draw out soft and subtle, it penetrated her nerves — "why, what do you think it is?"

She stood up, placed her hands on her hips, and stood looking at him transfixed, without answering. Again he burned with a sudden power.

"Well," he said, and his voice was so soft it seemed rather like a subtle touch, like the merest touch of a cat's paw, a feeling rather than a sound. "Well — I wanted to ask you to marry me."

March felt rather than heard him. She felt him everywhere — on her face, across her breasts, deep inside her, filling her and taking her soul. She was trying in vain to turn aside her face. A great relaxation seemed to have come over her, as though she had known this moment was coming and finally it had arrived. She stood silent, her head slightly on one side. He seemed to be bending towards her, invisibly smiling as he came for her. It seemed to her fine sparks came out of him, ready to jump across to her and burn through her skin.

Then very suddenly she said, "Don't try any of your tomfoolery on me."

A quiver went over his nerves. He had missed. He waited a moment to collect himself again. Then, after he had reconsidered his way of handling the matter, he said, putting all the strange softness into his voice, as if he were imperceptibly stroking her, "Why, it's not tomfoolery. It's not tomfoolery. I mean it. I mean it. What makes you disbelieve me?"

He sounded hurt. And his voice had such a curious power over her, making her feel loose and relaxed. She struggled somewhere for her own power. She felt for a moment that she was lost—lost—lost. The word seemed to rock in her as if she were dying. Suddenly again she spoke.

"You don't know what you are talking about," she said, in a brief and transient stroke of scorn. "What nonsense! I'm old enough to be your mother."

"Yes, I do know what I'm talking about. Yes, I do," he persisted softly, as if he were producing his voice in her blood. "I know quite well what I'm talking about. You're not old enough to be my mother. That isn't true. And what does it matter even if it was? You can marry me whatever age we are. What is age to me? And what is age to you? Age is nothing."

A swoon went over her as he concluded. He spoke rapidly—in the rapid Cornish fashion—and his voice seemed to sound in her somewhere where she was helpless against it. "Age is nothing!" The soft, heavy insistence of it made her sway dimly out there in the darkness. She could not answer.

A great exultance leaped like fire over his limbs. He felt he had won.

"I want to marry you, you see. Why shouldn't I?" he proceeded, soft and rapid. He waited for her to answer. In the dusk he saw her almost phosphorescent. Her eyelids were dropped, her face half-averted and unconscious. She seemed to be in his power. But he waited, watchful. He dared not yet touch her.

"Say then," he said, "say then you'll marry me. Say—say!" He was softly insistent.

"What?" she asked, faint, from a distance, like one in pain. His voice was now unthinkably near and soft. He drew very near to her.

"Say yes."

"Oh, I can't," she wailed helplessly, half-articulate, as if semiconscious, and as if in pain, like one who dies. "How can I?"

"You can," he said softly, laying his hand gently on her shoulder as she stood with her head averted and dropped, dazed. "You can. Yes, you can. What makes you say you can't? You can. You can." And with awful softness he bent forward and just touched her neck with his mouth and his chin.

Beneath his lips her pulse hammered, forcing blood through her lean, strong body. He felt weakness in her though, the weakness he knew he would use against her to bend her will to his. He moved his lips across her neck, letting the wetness from his mouth mark her as his. Although the mark would be gone, the effect of his mouth on her skin would remain and she would remember this sensation and her submission. She would never belong to another. Not as long as he lived and this wild fire consumed him. She panted and the gentle puffs of her breath caressed his cheek. The sweet vulnerability of her reaction stirred the master in him and the flames of his strength burned. His body became hot and ready, his groin was hard and unyielding as was his spirit. He pressed his hardness against her, letting her know her future with him.

"Don't!" she cried, with a faint mad cry like hysteria, starting away and facing round on him. "What do you mean?" But she had no breath to speak with. It was as if she was killed.

"I mean what I say," he persisted gently but cruelly, coming behind her to again hold his strong body against her weaker one. This time, he felt the softness of her hips. "I want you to marry me. I want you to marry me. You know that now, don't you? You know that now? Don't you? Don't you?"

"What?" she said. But her body was already responding to his, even against her will. Her heart thumped heavily, preparing herself for him and his intentions.

"Know," he replied, his voice a low growl in her ear.

"Yes," she said. She wanted to step away but if she turned around he would see the indecision in her eyes. "I know you say so."

He bit her lightly on the neck then lifted his head. "And you know I mean it, don't you?"

"I know you say so."

"You believe me?" he said, pushing against her and using his height to remind her of her weakness.

She was silent for some time. Then she pursed her lips in an effort to fight against the softness in her centre, but it was a waste of effort. The stirring deep inside her was as undeniable as her desire for his physical dominance.

But she couldn't trust her own thoughts, each notion in her mind was half-formed and wild. "I don't know what I believe," she said.

"Are you out there?" came Banford's voice, calling from the house.

"Yes, we're bringing in the logs," he answered.

March noticed how easily he could change his voice, speaking as though they had in fact been only attending to the logs and that everything was as it should be.

"I thought you'd gone lost," said Banford disconsolately. "Hurry up, do, and come and let's have tea. The kettle's boiling."

Finally, he released March and moved away from her. Instantly she felt his absence and a new emptiness settled inside her, making the soft heat of a moment before nearly unbearable. Even though she did not want to feel that hot longing, it had found her and had now become part of her life, a new craving that threatened to burn everything in its path. It would now be that desire, and not her own will, that dictated her actions.

She bent over to take some logs and the youth came up behind her and again pressed himself firmly against her backside. She felt his commanding hardness.

"I will have you, Nellie."

"Henry, I—" She tried to stand upright, but he held her down with one hand while gently stroking her hip with his other. His hand moved slowly, his fingertips seeking out the curves of her body and exploring the tender spot where hip turned into thigh. Although she tried to hide her body's reaction to his manly touch, her quick, uneven breathing caused her stomach to quiver. The youth growled. His slow seduction turned quick, and he shoved his hand under the hem of her tunic, moved it upwards and sought her bare skin.

His palm was rough and it rasped against the soft flesh of her lower back, leaving a trail of heat behind. He pressed his thumb to her spine and moved downward, as low as the band of her breeches would allow.

"I want you for my wife. You want me for your husband," he said, caressing the highest curve of her hips with the very tips of his fingers. She arched her back, aching for more of his light touch.

"I will give you what you need," he said. "You only have to say yes. Then you will have everything."

"I—I—" Her knees buckled, and he swung his arm around her waist to hold her upright then tugged her tightly to him. She tried to speak again but no words came.

"I've only just begun with this," he said and jerked his hips forward, demanding she acknowledge the hard press of his desire. "Understand?"

Still unable to speak, she simply nodded.

He released her slowly, giving her time to find her footing, then took an armful of little logs and carried them into the kitchen, where they were piled in a corner. March, after a moment to regain some of her composure, also helped, filling her arms and carrying the logs on her breast as if they were some heavy child. The night had fallen cold, and she felt the chill everywhere.

When the logs were all in, the two cleaned their boots noisily on the scraper outside, then rubbed them on the mat. March shut the door and took off her old felt hat—her farm-girl hat. Her thick, crisp, black hair was loose, her face was pale and strained. She pushed back her hair vaguely and washed her hands. Banford came hurrying into the dimly-lighted kitchen, to take from the oven the scones she was keeping hot.

"Whatever have you been doing all this time?" she asked fretfully. "I thought you were never coming in. And it's ages since you stopped sawing. What were you doing out there?"

"Well," said Henry, "we had to stop that hole in the barn to keeps the rats out."

"Why, I could see you standing there in the shed. I could see your shirt-sleeves," challenged Banford.

"Yes, I was just putting the saw away."

They went in to tea. March was quite mute. Her face was pale and strained and vague. The youth, who always had the same ruddy, self-contained look on his face, as though he were keeping himself to himself, had come to tea in his shirt-sleeves as if he were at home. March knew he ought not to eat that way, but she couldn't stop herself from watching the muscles of his forearms or the powerful ways his hands mastered everything they touched. He bent over his plate as he ate his food and she thought about his mouth moving over the soft neck of her skin.

"Aren't you cold?" said Banford spitefully. "In your shirt-sleeves."

He looked up at her, with his chin near his plate, and his eyes very clear, pellucid and unwavering as he watched her.

"No, I'm not cold," he said with his usual soft courtesy. "It's much warmer in here than it is outside, you see."

"I hope it is," said Banford, feeling nettled by him. He had a strange, suave assurance and a wide-eyed bright look that got on her nerves this evening.

"But perhaps," he said softly and courteously, "you don't like me coming to tea without my coat. I forgot that."

"Oh, I don't mind," said Banford, although she did.

"I'll go and get it, shall I?" he said.

March's dark eyes turned slowly down to look over his body, wondering if Banford could see the hardness of him. If he got up to fetch the coat, surely she would notice it then if she hadn't already.

"No, don't you bother," she said in her queer, twanging tone. "If you feel all right as you are, stop as you are." She spoke with a crude authority.

"Yes," said he, "I feel all right, if I'm not rude."

"It's usually considered rude," said Banford. "But we don't mind."

"Go along, 'considered rude'," ejaculated March, eager for an opportunity to fight against something, even a convention she typically paid no attention to. "Who considers it rude?" Once she had asked the question, she wondered at the young man's hardness. If she angered him enough to go after the coat, what then?

But Henry appeared unaffected by March's outburst. It was Banford who was most roused.

"Why, you do, Nellie, in anybody else," she said, bridling a little behind her spectacles, and feeling her food stick in her throat.

But March had again gone vague and unheeding, chewing her food as if she did not know she was eating at all. And the youth looked from one to another, with bright, watching eyes. He had moved forward, got closer to taking what he wanted.

Banford was offended. For all his suave courtesy and soft voice, the youth seemed to her impudent. She did not like to look at him. She did not like to meet his clear, watchful eyes, she did not like to see the strange glow in his face, his cheeks with their delicate fine hair, and his ruddy skin that was quite dull and yet which seemed to burn with a curious heat of life. It made her feel a little ill to look at him. The quality of his physical presence was too penetrating, too hot.

After tea the evening was very quiet. The youth rarely went into the village. As a rule, he read — he was a great reader, in his own hours. That is, when he did begin, he read absorbedly. But he was not very eager to begin. Often he walked about the fields and along the hedges alone in the dark at night, prowling with a queer instinct for the night, and listening to the wild sounds. He stalked through the woods, becoming even better at something he was already quite skilled at — hunting.

Tonight, however, he took a Captain Mayne Reid book from Banford's shelf and sat down with knees wide apart and immersed himself in his story. His brownish fair hair was long, and lay on his head like a thick cap, combed sideways. He was still in his shirt-sleeves, and bending forward under the lamplight, with his knees stuck wide apart and the book in his hand and his whole figure absorbed in the rather strenuous business of reading, he gave Banford's sitting room the look of a lumber camp.

She resented this. For on her sitting room floor she had a red Turkey rug and dark stain round, the fire-place had fashionable green tiles, the piano stood open with the latest dance music—she played quite well—and on the walls were March's hand-painted swans and water-lilies. Moreover, with the logs nicely, tremulously burning in the grate, the thick curtains drawn, the doors all shut, and the pine trees hissing and shuddering in the wind outside, it was cosy, it was refined and nice. She resented the big, raw, long-legged youth sticking his khaki knees out and sitting there with his soldier's shirt-cuffs buttoned on his thick red wrists. From time to time he turned a page, and from time to time he gave a sharp look at the fire, settling the logs. Then he immersed himself again in the intense and isolated business of reading.

March, on the far side of the table, was spasmodically crocheting. Her mouth was pursed in an odd way, as when she had dreamt the fox's brush burned it, her beautiful, crisp black hair strayed in wisps. But her whole figure was absorbed in its bearing, as if she herself was miles away. In a sort of semi-dream she seemed to be hearing the fox singing round the house in the wind, singing wildly and sweetly and like a madness. With red but well-shaped hands she slowly crocheted the white cotton, very slowly, awkwardly.

Banford was also trying to read, sitting in her low chair. But between those two she felt fidgety. She kept moving and looking round and listening to the wind, and glancing secretly from one to the other of her companions. March, seated on a straight chair, with her knees in their close breeches crossed, and slowly, laboriously crocheting, was also a trial.

"Oh dear!" said Banford, "My eyes are bad tonight." And she pressed her fingers on her eyes.

The youth looked up at her with his clear, bright look, but did not speak.

"Are they, Jill?" said March absently.

Then the youth began to read again, and Banford perforce returned to her book. But she could not keep still. After a while she looked up at March, and a queer, almost malignant little smile was on her thin face.

"A penny for them, Nell," she said suddenly.

March looked round with big, startled black eyes, and went pale as if with terror. She had been listening to the fox singing so tenderly, so tenderly, as he wandered round the house.

"What?" she said vaguely.

"A penny for them," said Banford sarcastically. "Or twopence, if they're as deep as all that."

The youth was watching with bright, clear eyes from beneath the lamp, his body on alert as though he might lose some ground and need to reclaim it.

"Why," came March's vague voice, "what do you want to waste your money for?"

"I thought it would be well spent," said Banford.

"I wasn't thinking of anything except the way the wind was blowing," said March.

"Oh dear," replied Banford, "I could have had as original thought as that myself. I'm afraid I have wasted my money this time."

"Well, you needn't pay," said March.

The youth suddenly laughed. Both women looked at him, March rather surprised-looking, as if she had hardly known he was there.

"Why, do you ever pay up on these occasions?" he asked.

"Oh yes," said Banford. "We always do. I've sometimes had to pass a shilling a week to Nellie, in the winter-time. It costs much less in summer."

"What, paying for each other's thoughts?" he laughed.

"Yes, when we've absolutely come to the end of everything else."

He laughed quickly, wrinkling his nose sharply like a puppy and laughing with quick pleasure, his eyes shining.

"It's the first time I ever heard of that," he said.

"I guess you'd hear of it often enough if you stayed a winter on Bailey Farm," said Banford lamentably.

"Do you get so tired, then?" he asked.

"So bored," said Banford.

"Oh!" he said gravely. "But why should you be bored?"

"Who wouldn't be bored?" said Banford.

"I'm sorry to hear that," he said gravely.

"You must be, if you were hoping to have a lively time here," said Banford.

He looked at her long and gravely.

"Well," he said, with his odd, young seriousness, "it's quite lively enough for me."

"I'm glad to hear it," said Banford.

And she returned to her book. In her thin, frail hair were already many threads of grey, though she was not yet thirty. The boy did not look down, but turned his eyes to March, who was sitting with pursed mouth laboriously crocheting, her eyes wide and absent. She had a warm, pale, fine skin and a delicate nose. Her pursed mouth looked shrewish. But the shrewish look was contradicted by the curious lifted arch of her dark brows, and the wideness of her eyes, a look of startled wonder and vagueness. She was listening again for the fox, who seemed to have wandered farther off into the night, and he was listening for the sound of her breath. Of course he would not be able to hear it from that far away, but that did not stop him from listening.

From under the edge of the lamp-light the boy sat with his face looking up, watching her silently, his eyes round and very clear and intent. Banford, biting her fingers irritably, was glancing at him under her hair. He sat there perfectly still, his ruddy face tilted up from the low level under the light, on the edge of the dimness, and watching with perfect abstract intentness. March suddenly lifted her great, dark eyes from her crocheting and saw him. She started, giving a little exclamation.

"There he is!" she cried involuntarily, as if terribly startled.

Banford looked round in amazement, sitting up straight.

"Whatever has got you, Nellie?" she cried.

But March, her face flushed a delicate rose colour, was looking away to the door.

"Nothing! Nothing!" she said crossly. "Can't one speak?"

"Yes, if you speak sensibly," said Banford. "Whatever did you mean?"

"I don't know what I meant," cried March testily.

"Oh, Nellie, I hope you aren't going jumpy and nervy. I feel I can't stand another thing! Whoever did you mean? Did you mean Henry?" cried poor, frightened Banford.

"Yes. I suppose so," said March laconically. She would never confess to the fox. Or to the idea that they were one and the same.

"Oh dear, my nerves are all gone for tonight," wailed Banford, setting the book in her lap with a sigh.

At nine o'clock March brought in a tray with bread and cheese and tea—Henry had confessed that he liked a cup of tea. Banford drank a glass of milk and ate a little bread. And soon she said, "I'm going to bed, Nellie, I'm all nerves tonight. Are you coming?"

"Yes, I'm coming the minute I've taken the tray away," said March.

"Don't be long then," said Banford fretfully. "Goodnight, Henry. You'll see the fire is safe, if you come up last, won't you?"

"Yes, Miss Banford, I'll see it's safe," he replied in his reassuring way.

March was lighting the candle to go to the kitchen. Banford took her candle and went upstairs. When March came back to the fire, she said to him, "I suppose we can trust you to put out the fire and everything?" She stood there with her hand on her hip, and one knee loose, her head averted shyly, as if she could not look at him. He had his face lifted, watching her.

"Come and sit down a minute," he said softly.

"No, I'll be going. Jill will be waiting, and she'll get upset if I don't come."

"What made you jump like that this evening?" he asked.

"When did I jump?" she retorted, looking at him.

"Why, just now you did," he said. "When you cried out."

"Oh!" she said. "Then. Why, I thought you were the fox!" And her face screwed into a queer smile, half-ironic.

"The fox! Why the fox?" he asked softly.

"Why, one evening last summer when I was out with the gun I saw the fox in the grass nearly at my feet, looking straight up at me. I don't know—I suppose he made an impression on me." She turned aside her head again and let one foot stray loose, self-consciously.

"And did you shoot him?" asked the boy.

"No, he gave me such a start, staring straight at me as he did, and then stopping to look back at me over his shoulder with a laugh on his face."

"A laugh on his face!" repeated Henry, also laughing. "He frightened you, did he?"

"No, he didn't frighten me. He made an impression on me, that's all."

"And you thought I was the fox, did you?" he laughed, with the same queer, quick little laugh, like a puppy wrinkling his nose.

"Yes, I did, for the moment," she said. "Perhaps he'd been in my mind without my knowing."

"Perhaps you think I've come to steal your chickens or something," he said, with the same young laugh.

But she only looked at him with a wide, dark, vacant eye.

"It's the first time," he said, "that I've ever been taken for a fox. Won't you sit down for a minute?" His voice was very soft and cajoling and his words were both invitation and challenge.

"No," she said. "Jill will be waiting." But still she did not go, but stood with one foot loose and her face turned aside, just outside the circle of light.

"But won't you answer my question?" he said, lowering his voice still more, forcing her to move closer to hear him.

"I don't know what question you mean," she said. There were so many questions between them—some that might never have answers.

"Yes, you do. Of course you do." He looked up at her and she saw the darkness in his eyes and the commanding twist of his mouth. "I mean the question of you marrying me."

"No, I shan't answer that question," she said flatly.

"Won't you?" The queer, young laugh came on his nose again. "Is it because I'm like the fox? Is that why?" And still he laughed.

She turned and looked at him with a long, slow look. Was his laughter mocking? Because he knew that when it came to her he would be getting what he wanted, regardless of her own intentions? All he had to do was touch her, press his body against hers again and her thoughts would scatter.

"I wouldn't let that put you against me," he said. "Let me turn the lamp low, and come and sit down a minute."

He put his red hand under the glow of the lamp and suddenly made the light very dim. March stood there in the dimness quite shadowy, but unmoving. He rose silently to his feet, on his long legs and moved to her. And now his voice was extraordinarily soft and suggestive, hardly audible. The sound seeped inside her, deep inside her and melting across her skin, washing her own essence away.

"You'll stay a moment," he said. "Just a moment." And he put his hand on her shoulder. She turned her face from him. "I'm sure you don't really think I'm like the fox," he said, with the same softness and with a suggestion of laughter in his tone, a subtle mockery. "Do you now?" And he drew her gently towards him and kissed her neck, softly. She winced and trembled and hung away. But his strong, young arm held her, and he kissed her softly again, still on the neck, for her face was averted. He opened his mouth and ran his moist lips across her feverish skin. He nipped her tender flesh, leaving a tiny trail of soft bites down to her shoulder. He moved his head to the other side and worked his way up, pressing her skin so tenderly between his teeth. The pressure of his teeth was light, yet she knew if she pulled away too soon he would leave a visible mark, a reminder of her weakness to him. So she stayed in his arms, letting him possess her with his mouth then — suddenly — with his lips across her own.

He pressed his mouth across hers and caressed her lip with his tongue. She gasped and he delved deeper, thrusting his tongue into her open mouth and demanding she submit to his forceful kisses. She sagged against him. He pulled her closer. Once she was flat against him, he stepped one of his lean legs between hers, forced her thighs apart and took hold of her hips. Finally, once she was shaking from his attack, he took away his mouth.

"Won't you answer my question? Won't you now?" came his soft, lingering voice. He kissed her cheek softly, near the ear, as he began grinding himself roughly against her. That wicked heat kindled and spread upwards. Oh, how easily he ignited it.

At that moment Banford's voice was heard calling fretfully, crossly from upstairs.

"There's Jill!" cried March, starting and trying to draw erect.

And as she did so, quick as lightning he kissed her again on the mouth, with a quick, brushing kiss. It seemed to burn through her every fibre. She gave a queer little cry.

He lifted his mouth and looked down into her face as he rubbed his hard body against her soft one. The heat he had awakened outside beside the wood pile hadn't gone. It had been simmering inside her. She hadn't realised it, but it was there simmering, wanting to burn—that heat, that undeniable heat. "You will, won't you? You will?" he insisted softly, staring into her eyes.

She stared back, but said nothing.

"Must you always know the consequences of not replying? Will you forever deny me only to force me to make you obey?" he asked. He grabbed the hem of her tunic and jerked it upwards. Her arms became tangled in the sleeves, her undergarments twisted. He jerked again, lifting the tunic higher and pulling until it came free then tossed it to the floor, only a foot from the flickering fire. The outline of March's breasts were visible through the thin chemise, and the youth stared at the pointed tips. He took one breast in each of his strong hands. "If you won't give yourself to me, then I will take you. It's what you want, even though you won't let the words come from your lips."

"Nellie! *Nellie!* Whatever are you so long for?" came Banford's faint cry from the outer darkness.

Henry lowered his hands and grasped her hips. He held her fast, pressing his hard, unyielding crotch against her, and was murmuring with that intolerable softness and insistency, "You will, won't you? Say yes! Say yes!" He began moving against her, starting a rhythm with his hips.

March, who felt as if the fire had gone through her and scathed her, and as if she could do no more, murmured, "Yes! Yes! Anything you like! Anything you like! Only let me go! Only let me go! Jill's calling."

He didn't let her go. Instead, he continued grinding against her, then rocking back and forth. The wet heat gathering deep inside her stole her breath, left her hanging in the space between awareness and mindlessness. The hot longing threatened to steal her last breath. She tried to pull away, but he kept moving against her, giving her what she needed. When she began to whimper, he covered her mouth with his own and kissed her firmly until at last the heat sparked and flashed and rolled deliciously through her. Her entire body shook and quivered, and she couldn't stand to look at him. He possessed her now, and she understood what she must say and do.

"You know you've promised," he said insidiously.

"Yes! Yes! I do!" Her voice suddenly rose into a shrill cry. "All right, Jill, I'm coming."

Startled, he let her go. She grabbed her tunic and slipped it on, the dull fabric again covering her breasts, and she then went straight upstairs, struggling with each step as she willed her legs to work in their usual manner.

Her night was long and restless and filled with dreams of both Henry and Banford. On this night though, when she awoke shaking and crying, Banford didn't stir. She slept soundly, her small chest rising and falling slowly. March managed to fall asleep again, but it was even more restless and disturbed.

Her last dream was of the young man, holding her tightly, pressing her back against the barn door, kissing her roughly while in the distance Banford was calling them in for tea. The youth was bare-chested, smelt of sawdust and was damp with sweat. Each time Banford called, he tugged her shirt higher and higher, until it was up and off and on the ground. Banford shrieked. The youth unbuttoned March's breeches. And when the calls were replaced by mournful wailing, the youth tugged down her breeches and undergarment and pressed himself against her. The coarse wood of the barn scraped against March's flesh, and the pain heightened her senses. The smell of him, the sound of his uneven breath, and the feeling of his body – it was everything and yet it wasn't enough.

Banford continued to wail, but March ignored the pain in her friend's voice. Instead of going to her friend, she stayed with him. She grabbed Henry's belt, worked it free and, as if her hands moved of their own accord, she began struggling with the button. Once it was undone, she pulled his pants down. She wanted him inside her. Deep inside. He took her hips in his hands and positioned himself in front of her. One hard, fast thrust and he would truly possess her. Instinct told her what to do. She spread her legs as far as the breeches — now at her feet — would allow. Then, knowing that the decision had been made and the moment had arrived, tensed and waited for him.

He stood before her, naked from the waist down, the evidence of his desire shocking, frightening and fascinating. She'd never had a man inside her before and was both terrified and wanton. She touched the tip of his stiff cock.

"It's yours, Nellie," he said, speaking in a low growl. "All you have to do is take it."

She continued to caress him, her fingers moving around the shaft.

"If you do not take it, I will give it to you anyway, as I know that is your desire."

He took her hand away and held it against the rough wood, high above her head. March squirmed, anxious and afraid, but she didn't pull away when he used his other hand to position that smooth tip between her legs. He rubbed it against her, started to slide it into her tight channel. Knowing he was finally going to take her, she dropped her head back and gave in.

But March awoke, shaking and shivering, with tears dampening her cheeks

In the morning at breakfast, after he had looked round the place and attended to the stock and thought to himself that one could live easily enough here, he said to Banford, "Do you know what, Miss Banford?"

"Well, what?" said the good-natured, nervy Banford.

He looked at March, who was spreading jam on her bread.

"Shall I tell?" he said to her.

She looked up at him, and a deep pink colour flushed over her face as she remembered everything from the evening before.

"Yes, if you mean Jill," she said. "I hope you won't go talking all over the village, that's all." And she swallowed her dry bread with difficulty.

"Whatever's coming?" said Banford, looking up with wide, tired, slightly reddened eyes. She was a thin, frail little thing, and her hair, which was delicate and thin, was bobbed, so it hung softly by her worn face in its faded brown and grey.

"Why, what do you think?" he said, smiling like one who has a secret.

"How do I know!" said Banford.

"Can't you guess?" he said, making bright eyes and smiling, pleased with himself.

"I'm sure I can't. What's more, I'm not going to try."

"Nellie and I are going to be married."

Banford put down her knife out of her thin, delicate fingers, as if she would never take it up to eat any more. She stared with blank, reddened eyes.

"You what?" she exclaimed.

"We're going to get married. Aren't we, Nellie?" And he turned to March.

"You say so, anyway," said March laconically. But she flushed and she, too, could swallow no more.

Banford looked at her like a bird that has been shot—a poor, little sick bird. She gazed at her with all her wounded soul in her face, at the deep-flushed March. The youth did not see Banford's expression. Or if he did, it meant nothing to him.

"Never!" she exclaimed, helpless.

"It's quite right," said the bright and gloating youth, sitting up straighter and reaching for another chunk of bread.

Banford turned aside her face, as if the sight of the food on the table made her sick. She sat like this for some moments, as if she *were* sick. Then, with one hand on the edge of the table, she rose to her feet.

"I'll never believe it, Nellie," she cried. "It's absolutely impossible!"

Her plaintive, fretful voice had a thread of hot anger and despair.

"Why? Why shouldn't you believe it?" asked the youth, with all his soft, velvety impertinence in his voice.

Banford looked at him from her wide, vague eyes, as if he were some creature in a museum.

"Oh," she said languidly, "because she can never be such a fool. She can't lose her self-respect to such an extent." Her voice was cold and plaintive, drifting.

"In what way will she lose her self-respect?" asked the boy.

Banford looked at him with vague fixity from behind her spectacles.

"If she hasn't lost it already," she said, looking across the table at March, a slight condemnation in her watery eyes. When her friend continued to remain silent, she looked back to the boy.

He became very red, vermilion, under the slow, vague stare from behind the spectacles.

"I don't see it at all," he said. He had finally stopped eating.

"Probably you don't. I shouldn't expect you would," said Banford, with that straying, mild tone of remoteness which made her words even more insulting.

He sat stiff in his chair, staring with hot, blue eyes from his scarlet face. An ugly look had come on his brow.

"My word, she doesn't know what she's letting herself in for," said Banford, in her plaintive, drifting, insulting voice.

"What has it got to do with you, anyway?" said the youth, in a temper.

"More than it has to do with you, probably," she replied, plaintive and venomous.

"Oh, has it! I don't see that at all," he jerked out.

"No, you wouldn't," she answered, drifting.

"Anyhow," said March, pushing back her hair and rising uncouthly. "It's no good arguing about it." And she seized the bread and the teapot and strode away to the kitchen.

Banford let her fingers stray across her brow and along her hair, like one bemused. Then she turned and went away upstairs, the sound of her footsteps fading quickly.

Henry sat stiff and sulky in his chair, with his face and his eyes on fire. March came and went, clearing the table. But Henry sat on, stiff with temper. He took no notice of her. She had regained her composure and her soft, even, creamy complexion. But her mouth was pursed up. She glanced at him each time as she came to take things from the table, glanced from her large, curious eyes — more in curiosity than anything. Such a long, red-faced, sulky boy! That was all he was. He seemed as remote from her as if his red face were a red chimney-pot on a cottage across the fields, and she looked at him just as objectively, as remotely.

At length he got up and stalked out into the fields with the gun. He came in only at dinner-time, with the devil still in his face, but his manners quite polite.

Nobody said anything particular. They sat each one at the sharp corner of a triangle, in obstinate remoteness. In the afternoon he went out again at once with the gun. He came in at nightfall with a rabbit and a pigeon, the rewards for his hunting efforts. At least he was able to show his skill in that way. Neither Banford nor March seemed to take notice of his offering and the resistance to appreciate his kill kept the red in his face. He stayed in all the evening, but hardly opened his mouth. He was in the devil of a temper, feeling he had been insulted.

Banford's eyes were red, she had evidently been crying. But her manner was more remote and supercilious than ever — the way she turned her head if he spoke at all, as if he were some tramp or inferior intruder of that sort, made his blue eyes go almost black with rage. His face looked sulkier. But he never forgot his polite intonation, if he opened his mouth to speak. March seemed to flourish in this atmosphere. She seemed to sit between the two antagonists with a little wicked smile on her face, enjoying herself. There was even a sort of complacency in the way she laboriously crocheted this evening.

When he was in bed, the youth could hear the two women talking and arguing in their room. He sat up in bed and strained his ears to hear what they said. But he could hear nothing, it was too far off. Yet he could hear the soft, plaintive drip of Banford's voice, and March's deeper note. He wished that March would tell Banford about the kisses, but he knew she wouldn't. He kept wishing for it though, the edges of his anger fading when he imagined the fog of outrage and disgust behind the Banford's spectacles. He was capable of stirring March beyond herself and that was something Banford would never be able to do. It was something she herself might never feel.

He wanted to storm into their bedroom and tell them both he and March were to be married and they both should accept the idea quickly and quietly. But the idea of stating yet again what was to happen was also insulting. Still, the anger in him stirred and churned.

The night was quiet, frosty. Big stars were snapping outside, beyond the ridge-tops of the pine trees. He listened and listened. In the distance he heard a fox yelping, and the dogs from the farms barking in answer. But that was not that he wanted to hear.

He got stealthily out of bed and stood by his door. He could hear no more than before. Very, very carefully he began to lift the door latch. After quite a time he had his door open. Then he stepped stealthily out into the passage. The old oak planks were cold under his feet, and they creaked preposterously. He crept very, very gently up the one step, and along by the wall, till he stood outside their door. And there he held his breath and listened.

Banford's voice. "No, I simply couldn't stand it. I should be dead in a month. Which is just what he would be aiming at, of course. That would just be his game, to see me in the churchyard. No, Nellie, if you were to do such a thing as to marry him, you could never stop here. I couldn't, I couldn't live in the same house with him. Oh—oh! I feel quite sick with the smell of his clothes. And his red face simply turns me over. I can't eat my food when he's at the table. What a fool I was ever to let him stop. One ought *never* to try to do a kind action. It always flies back in your face like a boomerang."

"Well, he's only got two more days," said March.

"Yes, thank heaven. And when he's gone he'll never come in this house again. I feel so bad while he's here. And I know, I know he's only counting what he can get out of you. I know that's all it is. He's just a good-for-nothing, who doesn't want to work, and who thinks he'll live on us. But he won't live on me. If you're such a fool, then it's your own lookout. Mrs Burgess knew him all the time he was here. And the old man could never get him to do any steady work. He was off with the gun on every occasion, just as he is now. Nothing but the gun! Oh, I do hate it. You don't know what you're doing, Nellie, you don't. If you marry him he'll just make a fool of you. He'll go off and leave you stranded. I know he will, if he can't get Bailey Farm out of us — and he's not going to, while I live. While I live he's never going to set foot here. I know what it would be. He'd soon think he was master of both of us, as he thinks he's master of you already."

"But he isn't," said Nellie.

Silence followed. The youth held tight to his breath as he wished again she would tell Banford about the kisses. He had mastered her and she knew it. Perhaps it didn't matter if she admitted it aloud. The truth was the truth.

"He thinks he is, anyway. And that's what he wants — to come and be master here. Yes, imagine it! That's what we've got the place together for, is it, to be bossed and bullied by a hateful, red-faced boy, a beastly labourer. Oh, we did make a mistake when we let him stop. We ought never to have lowered ourselves. And I've had such a fight with all the people here, not to be pulled down to their level. No, he's not coming here. And then you see — if he can't have the place, he'll run off to Canada or somewhere again, as if he'd never known you. And here you'll be, absolutely ruined and made a fool of. I know I shall never have any peace of mind again."

"We'll tell him he can't come here. We'll tell him that," said March.

"Oh, don't you bother. I'm going to tell him that, and other things as well, before he goes. He's not going to have all his own way while I've got the strength left to speak. Oh, Nellie, he'll despise you, he'll despise you, like the awful little beast he is, if you give way to him. I'd no more trust him than I'd trust a cat not to steal. He's deep, he's deep, and he's bossy, and he's selfish through and through, as cold as ice. All he wants is to make use of you. And when you're no more use to him, then I pity you."

"I don't think he's as bad as all that," said March.

"No, because he's been playing up to you. But you'll find out, if you see much of him. Oh, Nellie, I can't bear to think of it."

"Well, it won't hurt you, Jill, darling."

"Won't it! Won't it! I shall never know a moment's peace again while I live, nor a moment's happiness. No, Nellie —" And Banford began to weep bitterly.

The boy outside could hear the stifled sound of the woman's sobbing, and could hear March's soft, deep, tender voice comforting, with wonderful gentleness and tenderness, the weeping woman.

His eyes were so round and wide that he seemed to see the whole night, and his ears were almost jumping off his head. He was frozen stiff. He crept back to bed, but felt as if the top of his head were coming off. He could not sleep. He could not keep still. He rose, quietly dressed himself and crept out on to the landing once more. The women were silent. He went softly downstairs and out to the kitchen.

Then he put on his boots and his overcoat and took the gun. He did not think to go away from the farm. No, he only took the gun. As softly as possible he unfastened the door and went out into the frosty December night. The air was still, the stars bright, the pine trees seemed to bristle audibly in the sky. He went stealthily away down a fence-side, looking for something to shoot. At the same time he remembered that he ought not to shoot and frighten the women.

His blood stirred with the need to move, to conquer, so he prowled round the edge of the gorse cover, and through the grove of tall old hollies, to the woodside. There he skirted the fence, peering through the darkness with dilated eyes that seemed to be able to grow black and full of sight in the dark, like a cat's. An owl was slowly and mournfully whooing round a great oak tree. He stepped stealthily with his gun, listening, listening, watching.

As he stood under the oaks of the wood-edge he heard the dogs from the neighbouring cottage up the hill yelling suddenly and startlingly, and the wakened dogs from the farms around barking answer. And suddenly it seemed to him England was little and tight, he felt the landscape was constricted even in the dark, and that there were too many dogs in the night, making a noise like a fence of sound, like the network of English hedges netting the view. He felt the fox didn't have a chance. For it must be the fox that had started all this hullabaloo. The crafty fox with his beautiful coat, gleaming bright eyes, and brutal ways. The creature was as dangerous as he was elusive.

Why not watch for him, anyhow! He would, no doubt, be coming sniffing round. The lad walked downhill to where the farmstead with its few pine trees crouched blackly. In the angle of the long shed, in the black dark, he crouched down. He knew the fox would be coming. It seemed to him it would be the last of the foxes in this loudly-barking, thick-voiced England, tight with innumerable little houses.

He sat a long time with his eyes fixed unchanging upon the open gateway, where a little light seemed to fall from the stars or from the horizon, who knows. He was sitting on a log in a dark corner with the gun across his knees. The pine trees snapped. Once a chicken fell off its perch in the barn with a loud crawk and cackle and commotion that startled him, and he stood up, watching with all his eyes, thinking it might be a rat. But he felt it was nothing. So he sat down again with the gun on his knees and his hands tucked in to keep them warm, and his eyes fixed unblinking on the pale reach of the open gateway. He felt he could smell the hot, sickly, rich smell of live chickens on the cold air.

Then—a shadow. A sliding shadow in the gateway. He gathered all his vision into a concentrated spark, and saw the shadow of the fox, the fox creeping on his belly through the gate. There he went, on his belly like a snake. The boy smiled to himself and brought the gun to his shoulder. He knew quite well what would happen. He knew the fox would go to where the fowl door was boarded up and sniff there. He knew he would lie there for a minute, sniffing the fowls within. Then he would start again prowling under the edge of the old barn, waiting to get in.

The fowl door was at the top of a slight incline. Soft, soft as a shadow the fox slid up this incline, and crouched with his nose to the boards. And at the same moment there was the awful crash of a gun reverberating between the old buildings, as if all the night had gone smash. But the boy watched keenly.

He saw even the white belly of the fox as the beast beat his paws in death. So he went forward.

There was a commotion everywhere. The fowls were scuffling and crawking, the ducks were quark-quarking, the pony had stamped wildly to his feet. But the fox was on his side, struggling in his last tremors. The boy bent over him and smelt his foxy smell.

There was a sound of a window opening upstairs, then March's voice calling, "Who is it?"

"It's me," said Henry. "I've shot the fox."

"Oh, goodness! You nearly frightened us to death."

"Did I? I'm awfully sorry."

"Whatever made you get up?"

"I heard him about."

"And have you shot him?"

"Yes, he's here." And the boy stood in the yard holding up the warm, dead brute. "You can't see, can you? Wait a minute." And he took his flash-light from his pocket and flashed it on to the dead animal. He was holding it by the brush. March saw, in the middle of the darkness, just the reddish fleece and the white belly and the white underneath of the pointed chin, and the queer, dangling paws. She did not know what to say.

The youth wondered if March's chest was heaving with excitement, her eyes bright. Indeed, that would be the way she was, stirred by his skill. And Banford would be forced to thank him or endure the rudeness she so despised.

"He's a beauty," he said, standing straighter and looking down on the fallen animal. "He will make you a lovely fur."

"You don't catch me wearing a fox fur," she replied.

"Oh!" he said. And he switched off the light.

"Well, I should think you'll come in and go to bed again now," she said.

"Probably I shall. What time is it?"

"What time is it, Jill?" called March's voice. It was a quarter to one.

That night March had another dream.

She dreamt that Banford was dead, and that she, March, was sobbing her heart out. Then she had to put Banford into her coffin. And the coffin was the rough wood-box in which the bits of chopped wood were kept in the kitchen, by the fire. This was the coffin, and there was no other, and March was in agony and dazed bewilderment, looking for something to line the box with, something to make it soft with, something to cover up the poor, dead darling. Because she couldn't lay her in there just in her white, thin nightdress, in the horrible wood-box. So she hunted and hunted, and picked up thing after thing, and threw it aside in the agony of dream-frustration. And in her dream-despair all she could find that would do was a fox-skin. She knew that it wasn't right, that this was not what she should have. But it was all she could find. And so she folded the brush of the fox, and laid her darling Jill's head on this, and she brought round the skin of the fox and laid it on the top of the body, so that it seemed to make a whole ruddy, fiery coverlet, and she cried and cried, and woke to find the tears streaming down her face.

The night wasn't finished with her though. She had another dream.

The youth was there by the casket and took the fox away from poor lifeless Jill. He held the light tip of the tail in one of his strong hands and the neck in the other and wrapped the dead beast around March's shoulders. He pulled her away from the bare wooden coffin. He laid his mouth across hers and kissed her soundly. So soundly, her blood stirred and heat filled her. The tears became sweat that ran down her neck and between her breasts. Even though she ached to be held, he didn't pull her closer, he only held her with the fox and the possession of his mouth. March hated the stupid animal, and she grabbed blindly until she found its tail and wrenched it from Henry. He lifted his mouth. She threw the dead creature aside. It landed on the edge of Jill's coffin, the head dangling down, the mouth open in a mocking smile. March ran.

She ran outside, her legs churning inside her thin, white nightdress as she raced through the cold December air. It was dusk and the bare trees were shadowed in grey. The youth caught her at the top of the hill by the wood stack. He grabbed her and spun her around. His face was inches from hers, his cheeks red, eyes bright. Anger rolled off him in waves.

"She's gone now," March said. "You won."

He ignored her statement and once again pressed his mouth to hers. The roughness of the kiss did not surprise her but her body's response did. The anger inside him flowed into her, and she felt her body stir with hot blood and cruel need. She clung to the image of poor Banford, trapped in the stark wooden coffin. Hate him. He did this to her, she told herself, but the picture of her lost friend was not enough to stop her body's immediate response to the forcefulness of the youth. She parted her lips and let him invade her mouth.

He moved his mouth across hers and slid his hands around her waist then dropped them to grab her hips. The heat of his anger continued to flow into March, warming her body and sending waves of tension through her. The waves seemed to circle smaller and smaller, rolling tightly to her centre and settling there. She shifted to get more of the pressure his hands delivered to her hips and he laughed.

"You understand now what I want. How I'll know when I've truly won."

She wanted to tell him that she'd already known, that she'd wanted to give it to him. But now, with Banford gone, *it seemed wrong. Traitorous. And so March should move back and go to her dear friend's coffin. Instead she widened her stance and invited the hardness from between the youth's legs. He thrust forward and a bolt of heat shot upwards and she felt its effect all the way up into her breasts. Her nipples tightened into hard points and she ached for him to touch her as he had before.*

"Banford was right. I am your master."

Banford, her friend. Gone and never, ever coming back. Lost to her forever. March whimpered.

He thrust again, and she was lost for a moment, her mind clouded with shades of emotion much darker than the grey of the dusky night sky. She felt him lift her nightdress up to expose her knees then her thighs. When he lifted it higher, the cold night air whipped up between her legs, and the heavy mist in her mind evaporated. She thrashed against the youth, and he let go of the thin fabric and tumbled back. March spun and raced down the hill towards her poor lifeless friend.

The first thing that both she and Banford did in the morning was to go out to see the fox. Henry had hung it up by the heels in the shed, with its poor brush falling backwards. It was a lovely dog-fox in its prime, with a handsome, thick, winter coat—a lovely golden-red colour, with grey as it passed to the belly, and belly all white, and a great full brush with a delicate black and grey and pure white tip.

"Poor brute!" said Banford. "If it wasn't such a thieving wretch, you'd feel sorry for it."

March said nothing, but stood with her foot trailing aside, one hip out. Her face was pale and her eyes big and black, watching the dead animal that was suspended upside down. White and soft as snow his belly—white and soft as snow. She passed her hand softly down it. And his wonderful black-glinted brush was full and frictional, wonderful. Why hadn't she noticed that in her dream? She passed her hand down this also, and quivered. Time after time she took the full fur of that thick tail between her fingers, and passed her hand slowly downwards. Wonderful, sharp, thick, splendour of a tail. So much softer now in the light of day. She pursed her lips, and her eyes went black and vacant. Then she wrapped her hands around the neck before taking the head in her hand.

Henry was sauntering up, so Banford walked rather pointedly away. March stood there bemused, with the head of the fox in her hand. She was wondering, wondering, wondering over his long, fine muzzle. For some reason it reminded her of a spoon or a spatula. She felt she could not understand it. The beast was a strange beast to her, incomprehensible, out of her range. Wonderful silver whiskers he had, like ice-threads. And pricked ears with hair inside. But that long, long, slender spoon of a nose—and the marvellous white teeth beneath! It was to thrust forward and bite with, deep, deep, deep into the living prey, to bite and bite the blood. She wondered again at her dream, nearly wishing she could have the dream again, only with a different ending.

"He's a beauty, isn't he?" said Henry, standing by, the closeness of his lean, angular body stirring March's blood. It wasn't anger this time, she acknowledged. It was something else much harder to predict and control.

"Oh yes, he's a fine big fox. I wonder how many chickens he's responsible for," she replied.

"A good many. Do you think he's the same one you saw in the summer?"

"I should think very likely he is," she replied, forgetting herself as she caressed the dead animal with eager hands.

He watched her, but he could make nothing of her. Partly she was so shy and virgin, and partly she was so grim, matter-of-fact, shrewish. What she said seemed to him so different from the look of her big, queer, dark eyes.

"Are you going to skin him?" she asked.

"Yes, when I've had breakfast, and got a board to peg him on."

"My word, what a strong smell he's got! Pooo! It'll take some washing off one's hands. I don't know why I was so silly as to handle him." And she looked at her right hand that had passed down his belly and along his tail, and had even got a tiny streak of blood from one dark place in his fur.

"Have you seen the chickens when they smell him, how frightened they are?" he said.

"Yes, aren't they!"

"You must mind you don't get some of his fleas."

"Oh, fleas!" she replied, nonchalant.

Later in the day she saw the fox's skin nailed flat on a board, as if crucified. It gave her an uneasy feeling, a sensation that was oddly close to the one she'd felt during her dream. Even though the youth's efficient work impressed her, she said nothing to him and went about her chores as usual. No doubt he was thinking about more than the animal, but she left him to his dark thoughts.

The boy was angry. He went about with his mouth shut, as if he had swallowed part of his chin. But in behaviour he was polite and affable. He did not say anything about his intention. And he left March alone.

That evening they sat in the dining-room. Banford wouldn't have him in her sitting room anymore. There was a very big log on the fire. And everybody was busy. Banford had letters to write. March was sewing a dress, and he was mending some little contrivance.

Banford stopped her letter-writing from time to time to look round and rest her eyes. The boy had his head down, his face hidden over his job.

"Let's see," said Banford. "What train do you go by, Henry?"

He looked up straight at her.

"The morning train. In the morning," he said.

"What, the eight-ten or the eleven-twenty?"

"The eleven-twenty, I suppose," he said.

"That is the day after tomorrow?" said Banford.

"Yes, the day after tomorrow."

"Mm!" murmured Banford, and she returned to her writing. But as she was licking her envelope, she asked, "And what plans have you made for the future, if I may ask?"

"Plans?" he said, his face very bright and angry.

"I mean about you and Nellie, if you are going on with this business. When do you expect the wedding to come off?" She spoke in a jeering tone.

"Oh, the wedding!" he replied. "I don't know."

March stopped her sewing, briefly, and looked from one hot face to the other. Then she began stitching again.

"Don't you know anything?" said Banford. "Are you going to clear out on Friday and leave things no more settled than they are?"

"Well, why shouldn't I? We can always write letters."

"Yes, of course you can. But I wanted to know because of this place. If Nellie is going to get married all of a sudden, I shall have to be looking round for a new partner."

"Couldn't she stay on here if she were married?" he said. He knew quite well what was coming.

"Oh," said Banford, "this is no place for a married couple. There's not enough work to keep a man going, for one thing. And there's no money to be made. It's quite useless your thinking of staying on here if you marry. Absolutely!"

"Yes, but I wasn't thinking of staying on here," he said.

"Well, that's what I want to know. And what about Nellie, then? How long is *she* going to be here with me, in that case?"

Once again March ceased her stitching as the two antagonists looked at one another.

"That I can't say," he answered.

"Oh, go along," she cried petulantly. "You must have some idea what you are going to do, if you ask a woman to marry you. Unless it's all a hoax."

"Why should it be a hoax? I am going back to Canada."

"And taking her with you?"

"Yes, certainly." His cheeks had already turned red and his face was beginning to take on the tightness that had been there the night before. And in March's dream.

"You hear that, Nellie?" said Banford, the sharp gaze of her eyes piercing through the glass of her spectacles.

March, who had bent her head over her sewing, now looked up with a sharp, pink blush on her face, and a queer, sardonic laugh in her eyes and on her twisted mouth.

"That's the first time I've heard that I was going to Canada," she said.

"Well, you have to hear it for the first time, haven't you?" said the boy.

"Yes, I suppose I have," she said nonchalantly. And she went back to her sewing.

"You're quite ready, are you, to go to Canada? Are you, Nellie?" asked Banford.

March looked up again. She let her shoulders go slack, and let her hand that held the needle lie loose in her lap.

"It depends on *how* I'm going," she said. "I don't think I want to go jammed up in the steerage, as a soldier's wife. I'm afraid I'm not used to that way."

The boy watched her with bright eyes.

"Would you rather stay over here while I go first?" he asked.

"I would, if that's the only alternative," she replied.

"That's much the wisest. Don't make it any fixed engagement," said Banford. "Leave yourself free to go or not after he's got back and found you a place, Nellie. Anything else is madness, madness."

"Don't you think," said the youth, "we ought to get married before I go—and then go together, or separate, according to how it happens?"

"I think it's a terrible idea," cried Banford.

But the boy was watching March.

"What do you think?" he asked her.

She let her eyes stray vaguely into space, as though the answer might simply appear.

"Well, I don't know," she said, finally. "I shall have to think about it."

"Why?" he asked pertinently. He leant forward to stare hard at her, almost as though he hoped to make Banford vanish. If he couldn't see her, he could pretend she wasn't there.

"Why?" March repeated his question in a mocking way and looked at him laughing, though her face was pink again. "I should think there's plenty of reasons why."

He watched her in silence. She seemed to have escaped him. She had got into league with Banford against him. There was again the queer, sardonic look about her. She would mock stoically at everything he said or which life offered.

"Of course," he said, in his own mocking tone. "I don't want to press you to do anything you don't wish to do." Although he said nothing else, he made a point of looking her over, his keen gaze travelling up and down the length of her body. The memories of the rough kisses, his lean body against her softer one, her pounding heart and his hard desire, he knew that those thoughts were there with both of them. And so he did not need to say more. It was evident in the quick rise and fall of her breasts and the soft blush in her cheeks that she wanted things only he could give her.

The youth saw her response and believed that there was no room for compromise when it came to the question of marriage and living arrangements. It was his task to make sure she understood that his way was the only choice for them. He was her future and he could see no need to consider another path. He would do whatever was necessary to ensure his desires were met. And so he was content, at least for the moment, to return to his work, quietly, completing the task. March pursed her lips, picked up the dropped needle and with slow, careful motions returned to the sewing.

Banford wasn't done with the fight. "I should think not, indeed," she cried indignantly.

March continued the even motion of her stitches and the youth pretended not to hear. After a heavy, exaggerated sigh, Banford returned to her letter-writing. The remainder of the evening passed slowly.

At bed-time Banford said plaintively to March, 'You take my hot bottle up for me, Nellie, will you?"

"Yes, I'll do it," said March, with the kind of willing unwillingness she so often showed towards her beloved but uncertain Jill.

The two women went upstairs. After a time March called from the top of the stairs, "Good-night, Henry. I shan't be coming down. You'll see to the lamp and the fire, won't you?"

Despite everything, her words surprised him, and he sat for a long time, watching the fire burn down low.

* * * *

The next day Henry went about with the cloud on his brow and his young cub's face shut up tight. He was cogitating all the time. He had wanted March to marry him and go back to Canada with him. And he had been sure she would do it. Why he wanted her he didn't know. But he did want her. He had set his mind on her. And he was convulsed with a youth's fury at being thwarted. To be thwarted, to be thwarted! It made him so furious inside that he did not know what to do with himself. The impasse made him feel like a boy when he was certain he was now a man. But he kept himself in hand. Because even now things might turn out differently. She might come over to him. Of course she might. It was what she wanted and her business to do so. He knew this because he had felt the quick pace of her breath and the softness of her body.

Things drew to a tension again towards evening. He and Banford had avoided each other all day. In fact, Banford went in to the little town by the eleven-twenty train. It was market day. She arrived back on the four twenty-five. Just as the night was falling Henry saw her little figure in a dark-blue coat and a dark-blue tam-o'-shanter hat crossing the first meadow from the station. He stood under one of the wild pear trees, with the old dead leaves round his feet. And he watched the little blue figure advancing persistently over the rough winter-ragged meadow. She had her arms full of parcels, and advanced slowly, frail thing she was, but with that devilish little certainty which he so detested in her. He stood invisible under the pear tree, watching her every step.

And if looks could have affected her, she would have felt a log of iron on each of her ankles as she made her way forward. "You're a nasty little thing, you are," he was saying softly, across the distance. "You're a nasty little thing. I hope you'll be paid back for all the harm you've done me for nothing. I hope you will—you nasty little thing. I hope you'll have to pay for it. You will, if wishes are anything. You nasty little creature that you are."

She was toiling slowly up the slope. But if she had been slipping back at every step towards the Bottomless Pit, he would not have gone to help her with her parcels. Aha, there went March, striding with her long, land stride in her breeches and her short tunic! Striding downhill at a great pace, and even running a few steps now and then, in her great solicitude and desire to come to the rescue of the little Banford. The boy watched her with rage in his heart. See her leap a ditch, and run, run as if a house was on fire, just to get to that creeping, dark little object down there! So, the Banford just stood still and waited. And March strode up and took all the parcels except a bunch of yellow chrysanthemums. These the Banford still carried — yellow chrysanthemums!

"Yes, you look well, don't you?" he said softly into the dusk air. "You look well, pottering up there with a bunch of flowers, you do. I'd make you eat them for your tea if you hug them so tight. And I'd give them you for breakfast again, I would. I'd give you flowers. Nothing but flowers."

He watched the progress of the two women. He could hear their voices — March always outspoken and rather scolding in her tenderness, Banford murmuring rather vaguely. They were evidently good friends. He could not hear what they said till they came to the fence of the home meadow, which they must climb. Then he saw March manfully climbing over the bars with all her packages in her arms, and on the still air he heard Banford's fretful, "Why don't you let me help you with the parcels?" She had a queer, plaintive hitch in her voice.

Then came March's robust and reckless, "Oh, I can manage. Don't you bother about me. You've all you can do to get yourself over."

"Yes, that's all very well," said Banford fretfully. "You say, 'Don't you bother about me,' and then all the while you feel injured because nobody thinks of you."

"When do I feel injured?" said March, still moving easily as she spoke.

"Always. You always feel injured. Now you're feeling injured because I won't have that boy to come and live on the farm."

"I'm not feeling injured at all," said March.

"I know you are. When he's gone you'll sulk over it. I know you will."

"Shall I?" said March. "We'll see."

Banford continued to fret. "Yes, we *shall* see, unfortunately. I can't think how you can make yourself so cheap. I can't *imagine* how you can lower yourself like it."

"I haven't lowered myself," said March.

"I don't know what you call it, then. Letting a boy like that come so cheeky and impudent and make a mug of you. I don't know what you think of yourself. How much respect do you think he's going to have for you afterwards? My word, I wouldn't be in your shoes, if you married him."

"Of course you wouldn't. My boots are a good bit too big for you, and not half dainty enough," said March, with rather a misfire sarcasm.

"I thought you had too much pride, really I did. A woman's got to hold herself high, especially with a youth like that. Why, he's impudent. Even the way he forced himself on us at the start."

"We asked him to stay," said March, her steps stalling for the first time.

Banford stopped as well, her frail body stiff with indignation. "Not till he'd almost forced us to. And then he's so cocky and self-assured. My word, he puts my back up. I simply can't imagine how you can let him treat you so cheaply."

"I don't let him treat me cheaply," said March. "Don't you worry yourself, nobody's going to treat me cheaply. And even you aren't, either." She had a tender defiance and a certain fire in her voice.

"Yes, it's sure to come back to me," said Banford bitterly. "That's always the end of it. I believe you only do it to spite me."

They went now in silence up the steep, grassy slope and over the brow, through the gorse bushes. On the other side of the hedge the boy followed in the dusk, at some little distance. Now and then, through the huge ancient hedge of hawthorn, risen into trees, he saw the two dark figures creeping up the hill. As he came to the top of the slope he saw the homestead dark in the twilight, with a huge old pear tree leaning from the near gable, and a little yellow light twinkling in the small side windows of the kitchen. He heard the clink of the latch and saw the kitchen door open into light as the two women went indoors. So they were at home. Their home, so peaceful and tidy. Perfect for the two of them.

And so! This was what they thought of him. It was rather in his nature to be a listener, so he was not at all surprised whatever he heard. The things people said about him always missed him personally. He was only rather surprised at the women's way with one another. And he disliked the Banford with an acid dislike. And he felt drawn to the March again. He felt again irresistibly drawn to her. He felt there was a secret bond, a secret thread between him and her, something very exclusive, which shut out everybody else and made him and her possess each other in secret. Nothing else explained the moments they shared.

He hoped again that she would have him. He hoped with his blood suddenly firing up that she would agree to marry him quite quickly — at Christmas, very likely. Christmas was not far off. He wanted, whatever else happened, to snatch her into a hasty marriage and a consummation with him. Then for the future, they could arrange later. But he hoped it would happen as he wanted it.

He hoped that tonight she would stay a little while with him, after Banford had gone upstairs. He hoped he could touch her soft, creamy cheek, her strange, frightened face. He hoped he could look into her dilated, frightened dark eyes, quite near. He hoped he might even put his hand on her bosom and feel her soft breasts under her tunic again. His heart beat deep and powerful as he thought of that. He wanted very much to do so. He wanted to make sure of her soft woman's breasts under her tunic.

She always kept the brown linen coat buttoned so close up to her throat. It seemed to him like some perilous secret, that her soft woman's breasts must be buttoned up in that uniform. It seemed to him, moreover, that they were so much softer, tenderer, more lovely and lovable, shut up in that tunic, than were the Banford's breasts, under her soft blouses and chiffon dresses. The Banford would have little iron breasts, he said to himself. For all her frailty and fretfulness and delicacy, she would have tiny iron breasts. But March, under her crude, fast, workman's tunic, had soft, white breasts, white and unseen. So he told himself, and his blood burned.

He wanted to know more. Not only of her breasts, but of the softness between her legs. He would possess that as well. His hard body would be the perfect match for that softness and she would submit to him. Indeed it was that hardness that would allow him to truly master her.

When he went in to tea, he had a surprise. He appeared at the inner door, his face very ruddy and vivid and his blue eyes shining, dropping his head forward as he came in, in his usual way, and hesitating in the doorway to watch the inside of the room, keenly and cautiously, before he entered. He was wearing a long-sleeved waistcoat. His face seemed extraordinarily like a piece of the out-of-doors come indoors, as holly berries do. In his second of pause in the doorway he took in the two women sitting at table, at opposite ends, saw them sharply. And to his amazement March was dressed in a dress of dull, green silk crepe. His mouth came open in surprise. If she had suddenly grown a moustache he could not have been more surprised.

"Why," he said, "do you wear a dress, then?" He looked at her breasts, seeming so exposed now in that girlish garb. And her shoulders so suddenly delicate. And her neck, slender and swanlike. It was impossible that she would look that way, and he did not know if he liked it better or worse.

She looked up, flushing a deep rose colour, and twisting her mouth with a smile, said, "Of course I do. What else do you expect me to wear but a dress?"

"A land girl's uniform, of course," said he.

"Oh," she cried, nonchalant, "that's only for this dirty, mucky work about here."

"Isn't it your proper dress, then?" he said, feeling the heat and heaviness build in his groin as he wondered about this unexpected change in her.

"No, not indoors it isn't," she said. But she was blushing all the time as she poured out his tea.

He sat down in his chair at table, unable to take his eyes off her. Her dress was a perfectly simple slip of bluey-green crepe, with a line of gold stitching round the top and round the sleeves, which came to the elbow. It was cut just plain and round at the top, and showed her white, soft throat. Her arms he knew, strong and firm-muscled, for he had often seen her with her sleeves rolled up. But he looked her up and down, up and down.

Banford, at the other end of the table, said not a word, but piggled with the sardine on her plate. He had forgotten her existence. He just simply stared at March while he ate his bread and margarine in huge mouthfuls, forgetting even his tea. She was the same woman and then again she wasn't.

"Well, I never knew anything make such a difference!" he murmured, across his mouthfuls.

"Oh, goodness!" cried March, blushing still more. "I might be a pink monkey!"

And she rose quickly to her feet and took the teapot to the fire, to the kettle. And as she crouched on the hearth with her green slip about her, the boy stared more wide-eyed than ever. Through the crepe her woman's form seemed soft and womanly. And when she stood up and walked he saw her legs move soft within her modernly short skirt. She had on black silk stockings, and small patent shoes with little gold buckles. He wanted to touch the buckles, to feel the smooth corners and the sharp edges. Then he would run his hands up those stockings, up high and under the skirt. Then he would touch her between her legs. Would she mock him as she had the night before during her conversation with her dear, spectacled Banford?

No, she was another being. She was something quite different. Seeing her always in the hard-cloth breeches, wide on the hips, buttoned on the knee, strong as armour, and in the brown puttees and thick boots, it had never occurred to him that she had a woman's legs and feet. Now it came upon him. She had a woman's soft, skirted legs, and she was accessible. She had made herself accessible to him. No doubt that was her intention. He blushed to the roots of his hair, shoved his nose in his teacup and drank his tea with a little noise that made Banford simply squirm — and strangely, suddenly he felt a man, no longer a youth. He felt a man, with all a man's grave weight of responsibility. A curious quietness and gravity came over his soul. He felt a man, quiet, with a little of the heaviness of male destiny upon him.

She was soft and accessible in her dress. The thought went home in him like an everlasting responsibility.

"Oh, for goodness' sake, say something, somebody," cried Banford fretfully. "It might be a funeral." The boy looked at her, and she could not bear his face, so she turned sourly away from him.

"A funeral!" said March, with a twisted smile. "Why, that breaks my dream."

Suddenly she had thought of Banford in the wood-box for a coffin. And the fox wrapped around her neck. Then later, her running from Henry, racing through the darkness and from — what? Now, she couldn't remember what she had been racing towards. Or had she been racing away from something? Whatever it had been must not matter, for if it had, surely she would have remembered it.

"What, have you been dreaming of a wedding?" said Banford sarcastically.

"Must have been," said March, shifting in her skirt.

"Whose wedding?" asked the boy, taking the opportunity of speaking to her as a reason to look her up and down again.

"I can't remember," said March.

She was shy and rather awkward that evening, in spite of the fact that, wearing a dress, her bearing was much more subdued than in her uniform. She felt unpeeled and rather exposed. She felt almost improper. But at the same time a delicious power ran through her. If only she could label it and make use of it.

They talked desultorily about Henry's departure next morning, and made the trivial arrangements. But of the matter on their minds, none of them spoke. They were rather quiet and friendly this evening — Banford had practically nothing to say. But inside herself she seemed still, perhaps kindly.

At nine o'clock March brought in the tray with the everlasting tea and a little cold meat which Banford had managed to procure. It was the last supper, so Banford did not want to be disagreeable. She felt a bit sorry for the boy, and felt she must be as nice as she could. The plans for his departure made everything so much more pleasant.

He wanted her to go to bed. She was usually the first. But she sat on in her chair under the lamp, glancing at her book now and then, and staring into the fire. A deep silence had come into the room. It was broken by March asking, in a rather small tone, "What time is it, Jill?"

"Five past ten," said Banford, looking at her wrist.

Then not a sound. The boy had looked up from the book he was holding between his knees. His rather wide, cat-shaped face had its obstinate look, his eyes were watchful. His body, having made the shift from boyhood to manhood, felt different. Ready. Anxious. Tense. He wanted to leap up and shove Banford out of the room and up the stairs.

"What about bed?" said March at last.

Henry's body stiffened.

"I'm ready when you are," said Banford.

"Oh, very well," said March. "I'll fill your bottle."

She rose and headed across the room. Henry watched each sway of her hips and studied the way her skirt hem brushed across the stockings. When the hot-water bottle was ready, she lit a candle and went upstairs with it. Banford remained in her chair, listening acutely. March came downstairs again, still wearing the dress, stockings and shoes. The buckles caught the light of the fire and glimmered. He would touch her there first and take off the shoes. Then he might yank off the stockings. Or maybe he would tell her to take them off, slowly, while he was seated before her.

"There you are, then," she said. "Are you going up?"

Going and not coming. There was a certain difference in the words that meant everything.

"Yes, in a minute," said Banford. But the minute passed, and she sat on in her chair under the lamp.

Henry, whose eyes were shining like a cat's as he watched from under his brows, and whose face seemed wider, more chubbed and cat-like with unalterable obstinacy, now rose to his feet to try his throw. His heart thumped inside his chest, pushing hot blood through his veins. The heat in his upper thighs was nearly unbearable, so intense that all he could think of was easing it.

"I think I'll go and look if I can see the she-fox," he said, adjusting his trousers so that Banford could not see the effects of his musings about March. "She may be creeping round. Won't you come as well for a minute, Nellie, and see if we see anything?"

"Me!" cried March, looking up with her startled, wondering face.

"Yes. Come on," he said. It was wonderful how soft and warm and coaxing his voice could be, how near. The very sound of it made Banford's blood boil. "Come on for a minute," he said, looking down into her uplifted, unsure face.

And she rose to her feet as if drawn up by his young, ruddy face that was looking down on her. A wave of self-assured power rolled over him. Of course she would look at him that way. He was her master.

"I should think you're never going out at this time of night, Nellie!" cried Banford, her gaze sharp behind her spectacles.

"Yes, just for a minute," said the boy, looking round on her, and speaking with an odd, sharp yelp in his voice that he instantly regretted. He had meant for his voice to be low, calm and assured. It was the damn tension in his thighs and groin and the hot blood stealing his control.

March looked from one to the other, as if confused, vague. Banford rose to her feet for battle. Henry puffed out his thin chest and curled his hands into fists.

"Why, it's ridiculous. It's bitter cold. You'll catch your death in that thin frock. And in those slippers. You're not going to do any such thing."

There was a moment's pause. Banford turtled up like a little fighting cock, facing March and the boy. The logs continued to burn, and outside the wind continued to blow. Yet the three of them stood that way for too long, none of them ready to admit defeat. Finally Henry, whose blood continued to pound through his body, but now more from anger than desire, spoke firmly.

"Oh, I don't think you need worry yourself," he said. "A moment under the stars won't do anybody any damage." Then, to March, "I'll get the rug off the sofa in the dining-room. You're coming, Nellie."

His voice had so much anger and contempt and fury in it as he spoke to Banford, and so much tenderness and proud authority as he spoke to March, that the latter smoothed out her dress and touched her neck as she answered. "Yes, I'm coming."

And she turned with him to the door.

Banford, standing there in the middle of the room, suddenly burst into a long wail and a spasm of sobs. She covered her face with her poor, thin hands, and her thin shoulders shook in an agony of weeping. March looked back from the door.

"Jill!" she cried in a frantic tone, like someone just coming awake. And she seemed to start towards her darling.

But the boy had March's arm in his grip, and she could not move. She did not know why she could not move. It was as in a dream when the heart strains and the body cannot stir.

"Never mind," said the boy softly. "Let her cry. Let her cry. She will have to cry sooner or later. And the tears will relieve her feelings. They will do her good."

So he drew March slowly through the doorway. But her last look was back to the poor little figure which stood in the middle of the room with covered face and thin shoulders shaken with bitter weeping.

In the dining-room he picked up the rug and said, "Wrap yourself up in this."

She obeyed—and they reached the kitchen door, he holding her soft and firm by the arm, though she did not know it. When she saw the night outside she started back.

"I must go back to Jill," she said. "I must! Oh yes, I must."

Her tone sounded final. The boy let go of her and she turned indoors. But he seized her again and arrested her.

"Wait a minute," he said. "Wait a minute. Even if you go, you're not going yet."

"Leave go! Leave go!" she cried. "My place is at Jill's side. Poor little thing, she's sobbing her heart out."

"Yes," said the boy bitterly, looking her up and down in the way he often did, reminding her of the difference between them. He was angular, lean and demanding. She was soft, open and weak. "And your heart too, and mine as well."

"Your heart?" said March. He still gripped her and detained her.

"Isn't it as good as her heart?" he said, using his height to impose himself upon her. "Or do you think it's not?"

"Your heart?" she said again, incredulous.

She tried to back away from him, away from his towering form, but he moved with her. He would not let her go. Not then. Not ever.

"Yes, mine! Mine! Do you think I haven't *got* a heart?" And with his hot grasp he took her hand and pressed it under his left breast. "There's my heart," he said, "if you don't believe in it."

It was wonder which made her attend. Then she felt the deep, heavy, powerful stroke of his heart, terrible, like something from beyond. It was like something from beyond, something awful from outside, signalling to her. And the signal paralysed her. It beat upon her very soul, and made her helpless and as weak as he knew her to be. She forgot Jill. She could not think of Jill any more. She could not think of her. That terrible signalling from outside! And the fierce signalling from within herself. It was as though a switch had been turned and her own body had become foreign.

The boy put his arm round her waist and pulled her to him. She twisted and turned, trying to find herself, but he would not let her go. He used his knee to guide her legs apart then lifted his leg and pressed it into her crotch. Oh, the glorious pressure he supplied. It was everything she needed and wanted.

"Come with me," he said gently, lowering his leg and stealing away the delicious pain. "Come and let us say what we've got to say."

And he drew her outside, closed the door. And she went with him on wobbly legs down the garden path lit by the moon. That he should have a beating heart! And that he should have his arm round her, outside the blanket! She was too confused and needy to think who he was or what he was.

He took her to a corner of the shed, where there was a tool-box with a lid, long and low. Rays of yellow moonlight came in through the window.

"We'll sit here a minute," he said.

And obediently she sat down by his side.

"Give me your hand," he said.

She gave him both her hands, and he held them between his own. He was young, and it made him tremble. But she too was trembling. Not from the winter cold, but from anticipation.

"You'll marry me. You'll marry me before I go back, won't you?" he pleaded.

"Why, aren't we both a pair of fools?" she said.

He had put her in the corner, so that she should not look out and see the lighted window of the house across the garden. He wanted all of her, both her body and her mind, inside the shed with him.

"In what way a pair of fools?" he said. "If you go back to Canada with me, I've got a job and a good wage waiting for me, and it's a nice place, near the mountains. Why shouldn't you marry me? Why shouldn't we marry? I should like to have you there with me. I should like to feel I'd got somebody there, at the back of me, all my life."

"You'd easily find somebody else who'd suit you better," she said, fighting for a reason to say no.

"Yes, I might easily find another girl. I know I could. But not one I really wanted. I've never met one I really wanted for good. You see, I'm thinking of all my life. If I marry, I want to feel it's for all my life. Other girls, well, they're just girls, nice enough to go a walk with now and then. Nice enough for a bit of play. But when I think of my life, then I should be very sorry to have to marry one of them, I should indeed."

"You mean they wouldn't make you a good wife." She said the last words with a touch of bitterness, although she wasn't that sure why. Being a good wife wasn't a bad thing. But still, she resented these younger girls she'd never met. Ones who would be good for a bit of fun.

"Yes, I mean that," he said, not noticing the bitterness on March's tongue. "But I don't mean they wouldn't do their duty by me. I mean—I don't know what I mean. Only when I think of my life, and of you, then the two things go together."

"And what if they didn't?" she said, with her odd, sardonic touch.

"Well, I think they would." He thought about the situation with a new seriousness now that they had spoken so frankly and he'd finally had the opportunity to talk freely without the ever-present Banford censoring his every word. The heat in his body had cooled and been replaced by something else. But what it was he did not know. It was not anger, he knew that.

They sat for some time silent. He held her hands in his, but he did not make love to her. Since he had realised that she was a woman, and vulnerable, accessible, a certain heaviness had possessed his soul. He did not want to make love to her. Now that they had spoken and he had accepted the responsibilities, he shrank from any such performance, almost with fear. She was a woman, and vulnerable, accessible to him finally, and he held back from that which was ahead, almost with dread. It was a kind of darkness he knew he would enter finally, but of which he did not want as yet even to think. She was the woman, and he was responsible for the strange vulnerability he had suddenly realised in her. Her weakness, which had been the thing he most wanted her to expose, now frightened him.

"No," she said at last, "I'm a fool. I know I'm a fool."

"What for?" he asked.

"To go on with this business."

"Do you mean me?" he asked.

"No, I mean myself. I'm making a fool of myself, and a big one."

"Why, because you don't want to marry me, really?"

"Oh, I don't know whether I'm against it, as a matter of fact. That's just it. I don't know."

He looked at her in the dim light, puzzled. He did not in the least know what she meant. Her uncertainty matched his own. No, that wasn't quite it. He knew he wanted to marry her—that he did know.

"And don't you know whether you like to sit here with me this minute or not?" he asked.

"No, I don't really. I don't know whether I wish I was somewhere else, or whether I like being here. I don't know, really."

"Do you wish you were with Miss Banford? Do you wish you'd gone to bed with her?" he asked, as a challenge.

She waited a long time before she answered. "No," she said at last. "I don't wish that."

"And do you think you would spend all your life with her — when your hair goes white, and you are old?" he said.

"No," she said, without much hesitation. "I don't see Jill and me two old women together."

"And don't you think, when I'm an old man and you're an old woman, we might be together still, as we are now?" he said. He brushed his shoulder against hers then leaned against her.

"Well, not as we are now," she replied. "But I could imagine — no, I can't. I can't imagine you an old man. Besides, it's dreadful!"

"What, to be an old man?"

"Yes, of course." She was actually laughing just a bit and the light sound made him smile.

"Not when the time comes," he said. "But it hasn't come. Only it will. And when it does, I should like to think you'd be there as well."

"Sort of old age pensions," she said dryly, the small laughter gone.

Her kind of witless humour always startled him. He never knew what she meant. Probably she didn't quite know herself.

"No," he said, hurt.

"I don't know why you harp on old age," she said. "I'm not ninety."

"Did anybody ever say you were?" he asked, offended.

They were silent for some time, pulling different ways in the silence.

"I don't want you to make fun of me," he said.

"Don't you?" she replied, enigmatic.

"No, because just this minute I'm serious. And when I'm serious, I believe in not making fun of it."

"You mean nobody else must make fun of you," she replied.

"Yes, I mean that. And I mean I don't believe in making fun of it myself. When it comes over me so that I'm serious, then—there it is, I don't want it to be laughed at."

She was silent for some time. Then she said, in a vague, almost pained voice, "No, I'm not laughing at you."

A hot wave rose in his heart.

"You believe me, do you?" he asked.

"Yes, I believe you," she replied, with a twang of her old, tired nonchalance, as if she gave in because she was tired. But he didn't care. His heart was suddenly hot and clamorous and the tension was returning.

"So you agree to marry me before I go—perhaps at Christmas?"

She looked up at him and studied him with her careful eyes. Finally she responded, "Yes, I agree."

"There!" he exclaimed. "That's settled it."

And he sat silent, unconscious, with all the blood burning in all his veins, like fire in all the branches and twigs of him. He only pressed her two hands to his chest, without knowing. When the curious passion began to die down, he seemed to come awake to the world and the possibilities of adult desire.

"We'll go in, shall we?" he said, as if he realised it was cold.

She rose without answering.

"Kiss me before we go, now you've said it," he said.

And he kissed her gently on the mouth, with a young, frightened kiss. It made her feel so young too, and frightened, and wondering—and tired, tired as if

she were going to sleep. But that was not what she
wanted. She wanted certainty and strength, and so
pressed her body against him and kissed him with her
lips parted. She lifted one arm—forcing her breasts to
rise higher—and wrapped it behind his head. She
spread her legs and kept at him until the fear went out
of his kiss and his body became hard and unforgiving.
He kissed her, over and over, moving his mouth
across hers then thrusting his tongue deep into her
mouth, invading her, possessing her. Their breathing
turned to harsh puffs and gasps. Finally, she had to
pull away for a long, shuddering breath.

"I don't want to think of it," she said. "The only way
is for you to take what you want from me."

He kissed her again, this time without the gentle
beginning. Once she was again panting and sagging
against him, he grabbed the hem of her skirt and
jerked it up. The night air chilled her thighs, and the
skin above her stocking puckered but the cold did not
affect her desire. Still a liquid heat burned inside her,
making her channel hot and slick. The youth put his
hand between her legs and stroked. The night dreams
had prepared her for his touch and so she welcomed
the awkward touches, instinctively moving her hips,
trying to get more of what he offered. He found a
hidden spot between her legs and suddenly the
sensation was too much, too fierce, and she pulled
back.

"Be still," he said.

"But I—" She stopped because he silenced her with a
sharp glance from his blue eyes. The sudden change in
him mystified her. How could he go from frightened
to commanding? What did that mean for her? For her
future?

She might have wondered on it more, but he began to stroke the tiny spot between her legs, again with the same awkward motions but slower and gentler. This time, she remained still and the sweet heat circling her hips spread, taking over more of her body. Curious, she rocked her hips and was rewarded with a delicious intense heat, one that made her blood thick and her strong body soft.

"That's better," he said, his voice low. He shoved her back and flattened her to the rough wall of the shed. "Don't move until I release you."

March reached for his shoulders and braced herself. The quick flick of his fingers ignited flames deep inside her body and the burn worked through her, consuming her. There was no need to fight, soon enough she would belong to him. And so she gave herself over to him, letting the rings of tight pleasure and pain circle through her.

Soon, she began to shudder and gasp. The tight, hot sensation stealing her breath was foreign and frightening, but she had no control, no way to pull back from his possession. The coils wound tighter and tighter, until finally her body seemed to explode, tearing her apart from the inside. The youth continued to stroke her until she sagged against him, whimpering pitifully.

"Next time," he said, pulling her dress down, "you will make me feel that way."

* * * *

They went indoors. And in the sitting room, there, crouched by the fire like a queer little witch, was Banford. She looked round with reddened eyes as they entered, but did not rise. He thought she looked frightening, unnatural, crouching there and looking round at them. Evil he thought her look was, and he crossed his fingers.

Banford saw the ruddy, elated face on the youth — he seemed strangely tall and bright and looming. And March had a delicate look on her face. She wanted to hide her face, to screen it, to let it not be seen.

"You've come at last," said Banford uglily.

"Yes, we've come," said he.

"You've been long enough for anything," she said.

March looked at Henry's hands, now swinging at his sides as he marched into the centre of the room, and blushed, a bright red that told everything.

"Yes, we have. We've settled it. We shall marry as soon as possible," he replied, stopping with his shoulders squared.

"Oh, you've settled it, have you! Well, I hope you won't live to repent it," said Banford.

"I hope so too," he replied.

"Are you going to bed *now*, Nellie?" said Banford.

"Yes, I'm going now."

"Then for goodness' sake come along."

March looked at the boy. He was glancing with his very bright eyes at her and at Banford. March looked at him wistfully. She wished she could stay with him. She wished she had married him already, and it was all over. For oh, she felt suddenly so safe with him. She felt so strangely safe and peaceful in his presence. If only she could sleep in his shelter, and not with Jill. She felt afraid of Jill. In her dim, tender state, it was agony to have to go with Jill and sleep with her. She wanted the boy to save her. She looked again at him.

And he, watching with bright eyes, divined something of what she felt. It puzzled and distressed him that she must go with Jill.

"I shan't forget what you've promised," he said, looking clear into her eyes, right into her eyes, so that he seemed to occupy all herself with his queer, bright look.

She smiled to him faintly, gently. She felt safe again — safe with him.

But in spite of all the boy's precautions, he had a setback. The morning he was leaving the farm he got March to accompany him to the market-town, about six miles away, where they went to the registrar and had their names stuck up as two people who were going to marry. He was to come at Christmas, and the wedding was to take place then. He hoped in the spring to be able to take March back to Canada with him, now the war was really over. Though he was so young, he had saved some money.

"You never have to be without *some* money at the back of you, if you can help it," he said.

So she saw him off in the train that was going West — his camp was on Salisbury Plain. And with big, dark eyes she watched him go, and it seemed as if everything real in life was retreating as the train retreated with his queer, chubby, ruddy face, that seemed so broad across the cheeks, and which never seemed to change its expression, save when a cloud of sulky anger hung on the brow, or the bright eyes fixed themselves in their stare.

This was what happened now. He leaned there out of the carriage window as the train drew off, saying goodbye and staring back at her, but his face quite unchanged. There was no emotion on his face. Only his eyes tightened and became fixed and intent in their watching like a cat's when suddenly she sees something and stares. So the boy's eyes stared fixedly as the train drew away, and she was left feeling intensely forlorn. Failing his physical presence, she seemed to have nothing of him. And she had nothing of anything. Only his face was fixed in her mind — the full, ruddy, unchanging cheeks, and the straight snout of a nose and the two eyes staring above. All she could remember was how he suddenly wrinkled his nose when he laughed, as a puppy does when he is playfully growling. But him, himself, and what he was — she knew nothing, she had nothing of him when he left her.

On the ninth day after he had left her he received this letter.

Dear Henry,

I have been over it all again in my mind, this business of me and you, and it seems to me impossible. When you aren't there I see what a fool I am. When you are there you seem to blind me to things as they actually are. You make me see things all unreal and feel things wild and unnatural, and I don't know what. Then when I am alone again with Jill I seem to come to my own senses and realise what a fool I am making of myself, and how I am treating you unfairly.

Because it must be unfair to you for me to go on with this affair when I can't feel in my heart that I really love you. I know people talk a lot of stuff and nonsense about love, and I don't want to do that. I want to keep to plain facts and act in a sensible way. And that seems to me what I'm not doing. I don't see on what grounds I am going to marry you. I know I am not head over heels in love with you, as I have fancied myself to be with fellows when I was a young fool of a girl. You are an absolute stranger to me, and it seems to me you will always be one. So on what grounds am I going to marry you?

When I think of Jill, she is ten times more real to me. I know her and I'm awfully fond of her, and I hate myself for a beast if I ever hurt her little finger. We have a life together.

*And even if it can't last forever, it is a life while it does last.
And it might last as long as either of us lives. Who knows
how long we've got to live? She is a delicate little thing,
perhaps nobody but me knows how delicate. And as for me,
I feel I might fall down the well any day.*

*What I don't seem to see at all is you. When I think of
what I've been and what I've done with you, I'm afraid I am
a few screws loose. I should be sorry to think that softening
of the brain is setting in so soon, but that is what it seems
like. You are such an absolute stranger, and so different
from what I'm used to, and we don't seem to have a thing in
common. As for love, the very word seems impossible. I
know what love means even in Jill's case, and I know that in
this affair with you it's an absolute impossibility.*

*And going to Canada. I'm sure I must have been clean off
my chump when I promised such a thing. It makes me feel
fairly frightened of myself. I feel I might do something really
silly that I wasn't responsible for – and end my days in a
lunatic asylum. You may think that's all I'm fit for after the
way I've gone on, but it isn't a very nice thought for me.*

*Thank goodness Jill is here, and her being here makes me
feel sane again, else I don't know what I might do – I might
have an accident with the gun one evening. I love Jill, and
she makes me feel safe and sane, with her loving anger
against me for being such a fool. She is easy and accepts me
as I am. With her there is no challenge to change and face
things that are frightening and different. Well, what I want
to say is, won't you let us cry the whole thing off? I can't
marry you, and really, I won't do such a thing if it seems to
me wrong. It is all a great mistake. I've made a complete fool
of myself, and all I can do is to apologise to you and ask you
please to forget it, and please to take no further notice of me.*

*Your fox-skin is nearly ready, and seems all right. I will
post it to you if you will let me know if this address is still
right, and if you will accept my apology for the awful and*

lunatic way I have behaved with you, and let the matter rest.

Jill sends her kindest regards. Her mother and father are staying with us over Christmas.

Yours very sincerely,
ELLEN MARCH.

The boy read this letter in camp as he was cleaning his kit. He set his teeth, and for a moment went almost pale, yellow round the eyes with fury. He said nothing and saw nothing and felt nothing but a livid rage that was quite unreasoning. Baulked! Baulked again! Baulked! He wanted the woman, he had fixed like doom upon having her. He felt that was his doom, his destiny, and his reward, to have this woman. She was his heaven and hell on earth, and he would have none elsewhere.

Sightless with rage and thwarted madness he got through the morning. Save that in his mind he was lurking and scheming towards an issue, he would have committed some insane act. Deep in himself he felt like roaring and howling and gnashing his teeth and breaking things. But he was too intelligent. He knew society was on top of him, and he must scheme. So with his teeth bitten together, and his nose curiously slightly lifted, like some creature that is vicious, and his eyes fixed and staring, he went through the morning's affairs drunk with anger and suppression.

In his mind was one thing—Banford. He took no heed of all March's outpouring. None. One thorn rankled, stuck in his mind. Banford. In his mind, in his soul, in his whole being, one thorn rankling to insanity. And he would have to get it out. He would have to get the thorn of Banford out of his life, if he died for it.

With this one fixed idea in his mind, he went to ask for twenty-four hours' leave of absence. He knew it was not due to him. His consciousness was supernaturally keen. He knew where he must go—he must go to the captain. But how could he get at the captain? In that great camp of wooden huts and tents he had no idea where his captain was.

But he went to the officers' canteen. There was his captain standing talking with three other officers. Henry stood in the doorway at attention.

"May I speak to Captain Berryman?" The captain was Cornish like himself.

"What do you want?" called the captain.

"May I speak to you, Captain?"

"What do you want?" replied the captain, not stirring from among his group of fellow officers.

Henry watched his superior for a minute without speaking.

"You won't refuse me, sir, will you?" he asked gravely.

"It depends what it is."

"Can I have twenty-four hours' leave?"

"No, you've no business to ask."

"I know I haven't. But I must ask you."

"You've had your answer."

"Don't send me away, Captain."

There was something strange about the boy as he stood there so everlasting in the doorway. The Cornish captain felt the strangeness at once, and eyed him shrewdly.

"Why, what's afoot?" he said, curious.

"I'm in trouble about something. I must go to Blewbury," said the boy.

"Blewbury, eh? After the girls?"

"Yes, it is a woman, Captain." And the boy, as he stood there with his head reaching forward a little, went suddenly terribly pale, or yellow, and his lips seemed to give off pain. The captain saw and paled a little also. He turned aside.

"Go on, then," he said. "But for God's sake don't cause any trouble of any sort."

"I won't, Captain, thank you."

He was gone. The captain, upset, took a gin and bitters. Henry managed to hire a bicycle. It was twelve o'clock when he left the camp. He had sixty miles of wet and muddy crossroads to ride. But he was in the saddle and down the road without a thought of food. His mind was filled with images of Banford, hiding behind her spectacles, her thin lips flat and disapproving. Occasionally his mind's eye would fill with the image of Nellie, his future wife. And he would remember the way she looked in the dress on that last night and the way she'd softened at his touch. He knew how to manage her. It was Banford who was the problem.

* * * *

At the farm, March was busy with a work she had had some time in hand. A bunch of Scotch fir trees stood at the end of the open shed, on a little bank where ran the fence between two of the gorse-shaggy meadows. The farthest of these trees was dead — it had died in the summer, and stood with all its needles brown and sere in the air. It was not a very big tree. And it was absolutely dead. So March determined to have it, although they were not allowed to cut any of the timber. But it would make such splendid firing, in these days of scarce fuel.

She had been giving a few stealthy chops at the trunk for a week or more, every now and then hacking away for five minutes, low down, near the ground, so no one should notice. She had not tried the saw, it was such hard work, alone. Now the tree stood with a great yawning gap in his base, perched, as it were, on one sinew, and ready to fall. But he did not fall.

It was late in the damp December afternoon, with cold mists creeping out of the woods and up the hollows, and darkness waiting to sink in from above. There was a bit of yellowness where the sun was fading away beyond the low woods of the distance. March took her axe and went to the tree. The small thud-thud of her blows resounded rather ineffectual about the wintry homestead. Banford came out wearing her thick coat, but with no hat on her head, so that her thin, bobbed hair blew on the uneasy wind that sounded in the pines and in the wood.

"What I'm afraid of," said Banford, "is that it will fall on the shed and we shall have another job repairing that."

"Oh, I don't think so," said March, straightening herself and wiping her arm over her hot brow. She was flushed red, her eyes were very wide open and queer, her upper lip lifted away from her two white front teeth with a curious, almost rabbit look.

A little stout man in a black overcoat and a bowler hat came pottering across the yard. He had a pink face and a white beard and smallish, pale-blue eyes. He was not very old, but nervy, and he walked with little short steps.

"What do you think, father?" said Banford. "Don't you think it might hit the shed in falling?"

"Shed, no!" said the old man. "Can't hit the shed. Might as well say the fence."

"The fence doesn't matter," said March, in her high voice.

"Wrong as usual, am I!" said Banford, wiping her straying hair from her eyes. "If it hits the fence that'll be another repair. You'll be sawing and pounding either way."

March's gaze moved between her friend, the tree, and back. She had only wanted to get this chore done and now it was becoming more than a simple task.

The tree stood as it were on one spelch of itself, leaning, and creaking in the wind. It grew on the bank of a little dry ditch between the two meadows. On the top of the bank straggled one fence, running to the bushes up-hill. Several trees clustered there in the corner of the field near the shed and near the gate which led into the yard. Towards this gate, horizontal across the weary meadows, came the grassy, rutted approach from the high road. There trailed another rickety fence, long split poles joining the short, thick, wide-apart uprights. The three people stood at the back of the tree, in the corner of the shed meadow, just above the yard gate. The house, with its two gables and its porch, stood tidy in a little grassed garden across the yard. A little, stout, rosy-faced woman in a little red woollen shoulder shawl had come and taken her stand in the porch.

"Isn't it down yet?" she cried, in a high little voice.

"Just thinking about it," called her husband. His tone towards the two girls was always rather mocking and satirical. March did not want to go on with her hitting while he was there. As for him, he wouldn't lift a stick from the ground if he could help it, complaining, like his daughter, of rheumatics in his shoulder. So the three stood there a moment, silent in the cold afternoon, in the bottom corner near the yard.

They heard the far-off taps of a gate, and craned to look. Away across, on the green horizontal approach, a figure was just swinging onto a bicycle again, and lurching up and down over the grass, approaching.

"Why, it's one of our boys—it's Jack," said the old man.

"Can't be," said Banford, looking through her spectacles.

March craned her head to look. She alone recognised the khaki figure. She flushed, nearly rolling with a familiar heated desire, but said nothing. The inner heat swelled and surrounded her, wrapping itself around her shoulders with the weight of a shawl she'd put on again after a season.

"No, it isn't Jack, I don't think," said the old man, staring with little round blue eyes under his white lashes.

In another moment the bicycle lurched into sight, and the rider dropped off at the gate. It was Henry, his face wet and red and spotted with mud. He was altogether a muddy sight. March reached up and patted the wild locks of her hair and tugged on the front of her tunic. Some twigs and dry needles came loose and fell to the ground. It was no use, she looked a mess. Suddenly, she realised what a fool she was for fussing over her appearance and forced herself to drop her hands.

"Oh!" cried Banford, as if afraid. "Why, it's Henry!"

"What?" muttered the old man. He had a thick, rapid, muttering way of speaking, and was slightly deaf. "What? What? Who is it? Who is it, do you say? That young fellow? That young fellow of Nellie's? Oh! Oh!" And the satirical smile came on his pink face and white eyelashes, this time taking on a new and evil twist. March wanted to wipe the look off the man's face. What little there was between her and Henry was her business and nobody else's.

Henry, pushing the wet hair off his steaming brow, had caught sight of them and heard what the old man said. His hot, young face seemed to flame in the cold light and even from the distance they could see the red in his cheeks.

"Oh, are you all there!" he said, giving his sudden, puppy's little laugh. He was so hot and dazed with cycling he hardly knew where he was. He leaned the bicycle against the fence and climbed over into the corner on to the bank, without going into the yard. His entire body seemed to glow, and even though he'd only been gone little more than a week, he no longer moved like the boy March remembered. He moved like a man now and his effect on her was that much stronger. How had she not expected this? His return? Of course he would come back, hunting her down like a wounded rabbit, him the wild dog that saw her weakness and turned it against her.

"Well, I must say, we weren't expecting *you*," said Banford laconically.

March cast a glance at her friend, the truth of Banford's comment evident in the surprise flickering in her pale eyes. How little she understood, March realised.

The old man shifted on his weak legs, taking delight in the sudden awkward change in the circle beneath the dead tree.

"No, I suppose you weren't expecting me," said he, looking at Banford then at March, his gaze going slowly down and up her body even though the others were there. His eyes stayed too long on the curve of her breasts, now warm and heavy, newly aching for his touch.

She stood aside, slack, with one knee drooped and the axe resting its head loosely on the ground. Her eyes were wide and vacant, and her upper lip lifted from her teeth in that helpless, fascinated rabbit look. The moment she saw his glowing, red face it was all over with her. She was as helpless as if she had been bound. The moment she saw the way his body seemed to reach for her even though his arms remained at his sides. Her need was in her eyes and her desire lingered on her lips. He saw it plainly and knew by the way her chest suddenly rose and fell, that she had accepted the way he affected her.

"Well, who is it? Who is it, anyway?" asked the smiling, satirical old man in his muttering voice.

"Why, Mr Grenfel, whom you've heard us tell about, father," said Banford coldly.

"Heard you tell about, I should think so. Heard of nothing else practically," muttered the elderly man, with his queer little jeering smile on his face. "How do you do," he added, suddenly reaching out his hand to Henry.

The boy shook hands, just as startled. Then the two men fell apart.

"Cycled over from Salisbury Plain, have you?" asked the old man.

"Yes." Henry looked across the yard. Everything was the same as when he'd left--with the exception of March. She was different. Dark circles rimmed her eyes and she wasn't standing as close to Banford as he would have expected. In fact, the two of them were farther apart than he had even seen them stand. March had missed him, had clearly been affected by his absence, and that made him happy. Satisfied.

The old man smacked his hands together. "Hm! Longish ride. How long d'it take you, eh? Some time, eh? Several hours, I suppose."

"About four," he said, moving over to stand closer to Nellie. She looked up at him but said nothing. He felt the heat of her body and wished that the man would stop asking questions and that Banford would storm off in one of her sulks.

"Eh? Four! Yes, I should have thought so. When are you going back, then?"

He stood up to his full height and looked down at the old man. "I've only got till tomorrow evening."

"Till tomorrow evening, eh? Yes. Hm! Girls weren't expecting you, were they?"

And the old man turned his pale-blue, round little eyes under their white lashes mockingly towards the girls. Henry deflated and also looked round. He had become a little awkward. He looked at March, who was still staring away into the distance as if to see where the cattle were. Her hand was on the pommel of the axe, whose head rested loosely on the ground. He admired her strong fingers and remembered the way it had felt to have her touch him. He looked at her mouth and thought of their kisses. How could she have so easily cast him aside? And for what? Banford and an old man? This was to be her life? No. It wasn't and it was his responsibility to prevent her from wasting her years without him.

"What were you doing there?" he asked in his soft, courteous voice. "Cutting a tree down?"

March seemed not to hear, as if in a trance. She continued looking off into the distance. Oh! How he wanted to grab her, shake her and pull her away from this terrible scene. Anything to get her to see what she must do.

"Yes," said Banford. "We've been at it for over a week."

"Oh! And have you done it all by yourselves then?" he asked, again trying to draw March into the conversation.

"Nellie's done it all, I've done nothing," said Banford.

"Really! You must have worked quite hard," he said, addressing himself in a curious gentle tone direct to March. She did not answer, but remained half averted staring away towards the woods above as if in a trance.

"Nellie!" cried Banford sharply. "Can't you answer?"

"What—me?" cried March, starting round and looking from one to the other. "Did anyone speak to me?"

"Dreaming!" muttered the old man, turning aside to smile. "Must be in love, eh, dreaming in the daytime!"

"Did you say anything to me?" said March, looking at the boy as from a strange distance, her eyes wide and doubtful, her face delicately flushed.

"I said you must have worked hard at the tree," he replied courteously.

"Oh, that! Bit by bit." Her gaze travelled the length of his body. He brought himself up again, as he had when looking down at the old man. Then she continued, "I thought it would have come down by now."

"I'm thankful it hasn't come down in the night, to frighten us to death," said Banford.

"Let me just finish it for you, shall I?" said the boy.

March slanted the axe-shaft in his direction. He took the wooden handle slowly, using the exchange as an excuse to touch her. The muscles in his arm tightened, and her eyes widened.

"Would you like to?" she said, even though he was already holding the axe.

"Yes, if you wish it," he said. He wasn't really talking about the tree and they both knew it.

"Oh, I'm thankful when the thing's down, that's all," she replied, nonchalant.

"Which way is it going to fall?" said Banford. "Will it hit the shed?"

"No, it won't hit the shed," he said. No doubt she wanted it to strike the shed, as though getting rid of the building could erase what happened there. "I should think it will fall there—quite clear. Though it might give a twist and catch the fence."

"Catch the fence!" cried the old man. "What, catch the fence! When it's leaning at that angle? Why, it's farther off than the shed. It won't catch the fence."

"No," said Henry, "I don't suppose it will. It has plenty of room to fall quite clear, and I suppose it will fall clear."

"Won't tumble backwards on top of *us*, will it?" asked the old man, sarcastic.

"No, it won't do that," said Henry, taking off his short overcoat and his tunic. "Ducks! Ducks! Go back!"

A line of four brown-speckled ducks led by a brown-and-green drake were stemming away downhill from the upper meadow, coming like boats running on a ruffled sea, cockling their way top speed downwards towards the fence and towards the little group of people, and cackling as excitedly as if they brought news of the Spanish Armada.

"Silly things! Silly things!" cried Banford, going forward to turn them off. But they came eagerly towards her, opening their yellow-green beaks and quacking as if they were so excited to say something.

"There's no food. There's nothing here. You must wait a bit," said Banford to them. "Go away. Go away. Go round to the yard."

They didn't go, so she climbed the fence to swerve them round under the gate and into the yard. So off they waggled in an excited string once more, wagging their rumps like the stems of little gondolas, ducking under the bar of the gate. Banford stood on the top of the bank, just over the fence, looking down on the other three, the sun glinting off her spectacles.

Henry looked up at her, and met her queer, round-pupilled, weak eyes staring behind her round lenses. He was perfectly still. He looked away, up at the weak, leaning tree. And as he looked into the sky, like a huntsman who is watching a flying bird, he thought to himself, *If the tree falls in just such a way, and spins just so much as it falls, then the branch there will strike her exactly as she stands on top of that bank.*

He looked at her again. She was wiping the hair from her brow again, with that perpetual gesture. In his heart he had decided her death. A terrible still force seemed in him, and a power that was just his. If he turned even a hair's breadth in the wrong direction, he would lose the power.

"Mind yourself, Miss Banford," he said. And his heart held perfectly still, in the terrible pure will that she should not move.

"Who, me, mind myself?" she cried, her father's jeering tone in her voice. "Why, do you think you might hit me with the axe?"

"No, it's just possible the tree might, though," he answered soberly. But the tone of his voice seemed to her to imply that he was only being falsely solicitous, and trying to make her move because it was his will to move her.

"Absolutely impossible," she said, the words so soft the sound floated away on the breeze.

He heard her though. But he held himself icy still, lest he should lose his power over the moment and her.

"No, it's just possible. You'd better come down this way."

"Oh, all right. Let us see some crack Canadian tree-felling," she retorted, her frail shoulders stiff and her eyes flat with disdain behind her spectacles.

"Ready, then," he said, taking the axe, gripping it tightly in his fists as he looked round to see he was clear.

There was a moment of pure, motionless suspense, when the world seemed to stand still. Then suddenly his form seemed to flash up enormously tall and fearful, he gave two swift, flashing blows, in immediate succession, the tree was severed, turning slowly, spinning strangely in the air and coming down like a sudden darkness on the earth. No one saw what was happening except himself. He saw it and felt it in every muscle in his lean, hard body. No one heard the strange little cry which the Banford gave as the dark end of the bough swooped down, down on her. No one saw her crouch a little and receive the blow on the back of the neck. No one saw her flung outwards and laid, a little twitching heap, at the foot of the fence. No one except the boy. And he watched with intense bright eyes, as he would watch a wild goose he had shot. Was it winged or dead? Dead!

Immediately he gave a loud cry. Immediately March gave a wild shriek that went far, far down the afternoon. And the father started a strange bellowing sound.

The boy leapt the fence and ran to the fringe. The back of the neck and head was a mass of blood, of horror. He turned it over. The body was quivering with little convulsions. But she was dead really. He knew it, that it was so. He knew it in his soul and his blood. The inner necessity of his life was fulfilling itself, it was he who was to live. The thorn was drawn out of his bowels. So he put her down gently. She was dead.

He stood up. March was standing there petrified and absolutely motionless. Her face was dead white, her eyes big black pools. The old man was scrambling horribly over the fence.

"I'm afraid it's killed her," said the boy.

The old man was making curious, blubbering noises as he huddled over the fence. "What!" cried March, starting electric.

"Yes, I'm afraid," repeated the boy. "She is dead."

March was coming forward. The boy was over the fence before she reached it.

"What do you say, killed her?" she asked in a sharp voice.

"I'm afraid so," he answered softly.

She went still whiter, fearful. The two stood facing one another. Her black eyes gazed on him with the last look of resistance. Then in a last agonised failure she began to grizzle, to cry in a shivery little fashion of a child that doesn't want to cry, but which is beaten from within, and gives that little first shudder of sobbing which is not yet weeping, dry and fearful.

He had won. And it had happened almost without him trying, as though Fate had recognised what must occur and had made it so. March stood there absolutely helpless, shuddering – her dry sobs and her mouth trembling rapidly. Then, as in a child, with a little crash came the tears and the blind agony of sightless weeping. She sank down on the grass, and sat there with her hands on her breast and her face lifted in sightless, convulsed weeping. He stood above her, looking down on her, mute, pale, and everlasting-seeming. She was broken now and he would be the one to pull the pieces together. He alone could make her whole. He never moved, but looked down on her, watching and waiting for her to accept the truth of the situation. And among all the torture of the scene, the torture of his own heart and bowels, he was glad, he had won. In time, she too would be glad.

After a long time he stooped to her and took her hands. He pulled her close and held her tightly. There was no rush now to take what he wanted. She was his now and forever. He would have what he wanted from her every day and as often as he wanted.

"Don't cry," he said softly. "Don't cry."

She looked up at him with tears running from her eyes, a senseless look of helplessness and submission. So she gazed on him as if sightless, yet looking up to him. She would never leave him again. He had won her. And he knew it and was glad, because he wanted her for his life. His life must have her. And now he had won her. It was what his life must have.

But if he had won her, he had not yet got her. They were to be married at Christmas as he had planned, and he got again ten days' leave. They went to Cornwall, to his own village, on the sea. Each step he took through his village resounded with the thump of his success. The weight of his boots as he went across the stones of the streets reminded him of the weight of the tree boughs and of the frailness of Banford's body.

And so he enjoyed his time in the village. He took March's firm hand in his tough one and walked her through the streets, between the cottages and businesses, past the school, along the fenced farm lanes that bordered the centre of the village. With each new delight, her face brightened and she would turn to him, her dark eyes almost light with joy. He realised it was awful for her to be at the farm — so he took her away from it and showed her the sights of his village. But more than her delight, he relished her submission to him and his world. Years later, he would relive those days before the ceremony. On nights when his bed was cold and his heart felt like stone, he would draw up the images of March's smile, expectant and open, filled with the hope that he was going to take her pain away and replace it with something so hot it would burn away the loss of her best friend. During those hours when they walked hand in hand, scarves covering their chins, their heavy boots making dull thumps across the cold stones, she had believed he could mend her. And he had believed it. Why shouldn't he have? He had, with two strong swings of an axe, changed the course of their lives. He had planned, he had won. He could do anything.

Or so he believed.

On the eve of their wedding, the boy, still filled with confidence and the knowledge that he had won her, took his bride-to-be to the top of the highest hill in the village. He wanted her to see the dark hills, dotted with white and yellow lights. The moon was full and bright and the village was beautiful and when he looked across the valley he felt as if he owned it in the same way he would soon own her. He wasn't sure why he wanted her to see the expanse of homes and farms, but he did. The highest place was the centre point of the cemetery and so they were surrounded by grave markers and low trees.

To the left were recent graves — one that looked to have been covered in late autumn and one, still a hole, that looked to have been forgotten. The edges of the one abandoned were not sharp from being freshly dug. They were soft from the rain and snow and now the hole gaped open like a mouth waiting to devour someone.

March pointed to the hole. "Odd, isn't it? An empty hole like that? Why go to the trouble of digging it if it's not needed?"

The boy ignored her enquiries as he wrapped his arm behind her back and turned her to face the other way. "The large farm there, do you see it? That's the home of Captain Berryman."

"Who?"

"The captain who gave me the leave to go to you. After I received your letter I went straight to him. He let me go even though I hadn't earned the time away."

"I didn't realise the letter was going to have such an effect on you," she said, her gaze on the fencing connecting the captain's outbuildings. "I expected you to do the sensible thing and just throw it away and forget about me."

The image of Banford standing in the path of the tree flashed in his mind and again he was reminded that he had won and he knew the satisfaction of getting what he wanted. "I never even considered giving up on what I wanted," he said, tightening his grip around her back.

She looked up at him and her dark eyes caught the gleam of the moonlight. He'd never seen her more weak and beautiful. "I suppose I should stop by and thank him for letting you leave. Shouldn't I?"

But Henry barely heard her, and so he did not respond. He was instead reliving Banford's last moments, remembering the mocking tilt of her small head and the crack of the tree as it fell from the second swing.

They stood in silence for a while, their breaths coming out in cold puffs that became a delicate fog and filled the air in front of them. He watched the gentle rise and fall of her chest and thought about seducing her as he had before, pressing himself against her until she softened and gave in, but decided to wait. Once they were husband and wife it would no longer be seduction, it would be her submission and his control. And taking her now would deny him the opportunity to revel in his last hours as victor.

The wind picked up and crept under their scarves and iced their cheeks. And so it became too cold to stand on the hill. Henry dropped his arm from behind her back and took her hand. "Let's go," he said. She took one last look at the view and turned to the graves behind them.

Suddenly impatient for the night to end, he pulled her forward and they neared the empty hole. March stopped at the foot of it and looked across the soft edges and again toward the captain's farm far away in the valley. "It really is odd, isn't it?" she said. "To dig a grave but not use it. What do you think it means?"

Henry heard her questions that time but he did not want to reply. So he tugged her forward, leading her away. He had accomplished what he set out to do and saw no reason to linger.

Their first night as husband and wife they ate a fine meal prepared by the pastor's wife. He had rented some rooms for them at an inn and she had brought the meal to them. She was a kind woman who seemed to see the best in everyone. She cooked them a fine leg of lamb and some spiced potatoes. She even made them a small, white wedding cake.

Even though he kept waiting, the woman never asked any questions as she set up the meal. Not any that were difficult to answer anyway, such as, 'How did you two meet?' That one especially would lead to another and another then they would be faced with the death of Banford, yet again. She, especially, was the one person he did not want to invade, the night when he finally mastered Nellie. But he was filled with uncertainty and could not decide how best to proceed in taking from his new wife what was now rightly his. It was as though he wanted to do it in a rush, all at once and be done with it, yet at the same time he wanted his coupling with Nellie to last forever. And so the meal, which they ate in front of the fireplace in the centre of the room, was a surprise to Henry. It was a welcome one though, because the meal gave him the opportunity to observe the woman newly made his wife and decide how he should treat her. He studied her while they ate.

She wore the green dress and black stockings and fine black shoes with buckles. She looked as womanly as she had the first time he had seen her in the attire, and he appreciated the reminder of that night.

"I'm glad you wore the dress," he said, after swallowing a mouthful of tender lamb.

"Remember the last time I wore it?" she asked, her gaze down on the sweet meat covering her plate. She had yet to eat much even though his plate was nearly empty.

"I do." He lowered his voice and tried a soft smile. "But that wasn't what I was thinking of."

"It *is* what I was thinking of." She moved her potatoes around the plate with her fork and finally looked up, and he saw the weight of the loss of Banford in her dark eyes. She blinked away a single tear. "I can't stop thinking of it."

"You must stop thinking of the farm." He pierced another piece of lamb and put it into his mouth, chewing slowly and thoroughly and relishing how easily he had removed Banford from their lives. Yet her ghost lingered, haunting them. If he only could grab the visage, squeeze it until it evaporated and be done with her once and for all. After he swallowed the pulverised meat, he said, "And you must stop thinking of her. It's the only way."

March dropped her fork onto the table. "But she —"

Henry leapt from his chair so quickly it toppled behind him. The hefty smack of the wood made Nellie jump and her eyes brighten. Although he hadn't intended to frighten her, he was glad for it because he liked to see her that way. Her eyes wide, her breasts rising and falling quickly, and her fingers gripping the edge of the table. She was vulnerable and weak. He was manly and in charge.

He grabbed one of her arms and tugged. "Stand, Nellie. I intend to have you now."

She stood on quivering legs. He kicked her chair away, and she jumped when it too thumped to the floor.

"Is it the noise that frightens you? Or is it me?"

She turned and her gaze darted to the chair then back to him. "The farm was quiet. Very quiet. I think the only sound that ever affected me there was the screech of the chickens when the fox was after them."

Henry remembered the screech of Banford's cries of anguish and anger. Those were the sounds that had made his skin tight with emotion. He took Nellie's other arm and pulled her away from the table. "You aren't at the farm now. You're with me, and you're mine."

"I know." She didn't look at him.

"Your life didn't start at the farm. It didn't start with Banford."

"I know."

"You know, but what are you going to do about it?"

He wondered if she was going to say it—'You killed Banford, my beloved Banford.'

He waited in silence, gripping her arms tight enough to feel the bones within. If she did mention her dear, frail, bespectacled friend he didn't know what he would do. Or rather he was afraid of what he might do.

Finally, she looked at him. The flames of the fire cast a golden glow across her face, and so her usual firm expression was softened. But it was her eyes where he saw the difference. He saw that she was trying to forget Banford. She was trying to be his and only his. His fear that she would drag her friend into their wedding night faded. He lifted his mouth into the curve of a smile. She did not smile back but she did not look away.

"Lift your face more so that I can kiss you."

She did as he had requested, and he kissed her soundly. The gentle warmth of her lips stirred his blood, and this time he was determined to see things through to the end, to show her why he was her master. He lifted his mouth from hers, wrapped his arms around her waist and lifted her. He threw her over his shoulder and gripped her stockinged legs. The gold buckles of her shoes gleamed in the firelight. She was light and willing, so carrying her to their marriage bedroom was as easy as carrying a sack of chicken feed to the shed.

Once he had positioned himself at the foot of the bed, he threw her across it. She rolled onto her side and moved to the edge of the mattress.

"No. I want you on the bed. Lift your skirt."

She rolled onto her back. Again she did as he had asked but no more. "Lift it higher. And take off your stockings."

She pulled the hem of her dress high on her thighs to expose the garters. He watched, fascinated, as her strong fingers worked over the tabs and freed the stockings from the straps. "Wait," he said when she started to unroll the stockings.

He crawled onto the bed, positioned himself between her legs and placed his hands at the top of one thigh. Her skin was soft, much softer than he had ever imagined. How could a woman so strong, with muscles so firm, have such soft, smooth skin? It was incomprehensible to him. And so he ran his hands down her leg, taking the stocking down and off. Instead of removing the stocking from the other leg, he placed his mouth on the thigh he had just exposed. He ran his mouth upwards, inching his way to the warm juncture between her legs. The musky scent of her arousal filled his nostrils, awakening the feral part of him. He covered her mound with his mouth, speared his tongue between her slick nether lips. The taste of her coated his tongue and so he lapped the sweet liquid. Beneath him, she squirmed but did not move away. Again and again, he licked the tiny bud, working her into a fierce frenzy. But he would not release her so soon. He wanted her desperate and needy when he finally drove his cock into her.

He lifted his mouth and turned his attention to the other leg. She lifted her head to watch him, her body motionless. Her stillness appealed to him, and he felt himself responding, growing hotter and harder, preparing to thrust into her.

The flames in the bedroom fireplace flickered and danced and cast shadows across her pale skin. He threw the second stocking aside, sat up and folded his arms across his chest, holding himself back to savour the moment. "Stand up and take your dress off."

After rolling to her feet, she started on the tiny buttons of her dress. Her obedient efficiency aroused him even more. She would do his bidding and be glad for it. Once the dress had been cast onto a chair, he told her to take off her slip and stand before him naked. She complied. He unfolded his arms, and stretched out onto his back to take off his own clothing. Piece by piece it fell to the floor in a pile.

Once he was naked, he thrust his hips upwards. "Look at me, Nellie. And while you look at me, touch yourself as I touched you."

Only her eyelids moved. She blinked twice.

Henry grabbed his shaft and stroked himself. "Do as I say."

Slowly, she slipped one hand between her legs and began caressing herself.

"More," he commanded, gliding his hand up and down as he watched her.

Gradually she accepted his stare and allowed herself to move faster. When she dropped her head back and closed her eyes, he got off the bed. He turned her around, pushed her back onto the quilt and then climbed on top of her. He kissed her and ran his mouth down the smooth column of her throat. He worked his way lower until his mouth lingered above one of her nipples. He licked the tight tip, making her moan and lift her back off the mattress as she tried to shove more of her breast into his mouth. He parted his lips further and took in as much of her warm mound as he could. She set her hands on the sides of his head and then slid her fingers through his hair. When her grip eased, he knew she was close to the precipice and so lifted his mouth.

He braced himself above her, his knees between hers. "Spread your legs, Nellie."

She did.

"Who do you belong to?"

Her reply came out as a whisper. "You."

Staring down at her so that she could feel his dominance, he said, "Say my name."

"Henry Grenfel." Her brown eyes were hazed with desire and desperate need. "I belong to you, Henry Grenfel."

And she always would.

He impaled her. She winced. He paused, waiting for her body to soften and accept him as its master. The moment seemed to last much longer than the seconds that actually passed, but he held steady, feeling her cunt become slick around his stiff cock. "Do you want me?" he asked after she began to whimper and squirm beneath him.

"Yes. Yes, Henry."

He grabbed the sheets in his fists and began to move his hips slowly, sliding his hard shaft in and out. She grabbed his shoulders and thrust against him. When he increased his speed, she turned her face to the side. He was glad she'd looked away. It allowed him time to stare at her face and watch her expression as he conquered her.

The flames of the fire cast a yellowish hue across her and made her dark hair glow. The strands lay across the pillow, curving downward towards the bed, a series of delicate arrows. He thrust harder, watching the arrows. The strands shifted, yet remained pointing downward, to the bed, to the place where their bodies were fused. As he continued to move into her, her mouth opened and she began to pant, as though she'd been chased through the woods and had finally found a place to hide. But of course, that was not true. She would never have a place to hide.

"Say it again. Tell me who owns you."

She opened her eyes and her gaze was hazy as she looked up into his face. "I—I…"

To remind her, he drove his cock into her cunt, thrusting himself in to the hilt. But when she remained silent he stopped. She would say the words or get no more.

"You, Henry. I belong to you, Henry Grenfel."

The boy was satisfied and so he impaled her again with his stiff shaft.

March welcomed Henry's possession. His body took command of hers and she went willingly, letting him drive into her with unrelenting fury. Soon her body coiled with a hot tension that squeezed the last of her away. It was as though she ceased existing, maybe that she had never really existed at all. As she felt the rings of harsh pleasure subside, she felt she was both alive and dead. She had never felt more alive, filled with energy and hope, and yet she had never felt more dead, as though everything she had ever been meant to do was now done.

Above her, Henry moaned as he continued to rock back and forth. He emptied himself into her and then collapsed upon her with a grunt. He said nothing and she was glad for that because she had nothing left to say to him.

She closed her eyes and slept.

The next morning, her new husband woke her with a soft row of kisses across her back. The light press of his mouth stirred her blood, and she waited for the searing rush of desire she'd felt the night before. But it did not come. After she stirred, he rolled her onto her back and used his knee to spread her thighs. She expected that hot rush of need to wash over her and remove her conscious thoughts, but it did not find her. Instead, she simply felt a warm flush of expectation.

As he had the night before, he positioned himself between her legs and entered her with one thrust. Once he was fully inside, he paused, waiting for her body to once again adjust to his thick invasion. March opened her eyes and stared at a crack in the plaster above. The early sunlight spread across the ceiling, casting the shadows of a new day, the first of her new life as Mrs Grenfel.

Henry didn't kiss her while he waited for her body to soften and turn wet. Instead, he rolled his hips gently against her, reminding her of his physical dominance. "You are mine. Today and every day that follows."

"I know," she replied. It was what she wanted. It must be, she told herself as she waited for that wild rush of heat to steal her senses.

Then he pulled back his body back, leaving her cunt empty, and looked down, the morning sun so bright on his face that his mouth looked harsh. "And I'll take you whenever I want." He lowered his mouth to one of her breasts and sucked her nipple. When it tightened into an obedient peak, he tended to the other breast, working it until it too responded. Once he was satisfied, he loomed above her and added, "I'll take you however I want."

"Yes, she said, spreading her legs.

"No. Roll over."

She stared up at him, confused.

"Onto your stomach."

Wanting to satisfy him, she rolled over and then cocked her head to see him. He was looking not at her face but was staring at her naked hips. His cock was stiff and jutting forward. He reached under her and lifted her body until her hips were pressed against his groin. She felt the press of his shaft and remembered that night in the shed when he'd first brought up the question of marriage. She clung to the memory of how her body had responded, getting hot and wet between her legs when he'd pressed himself against her.

He placed the smooth tip of his cock between her legs and used his hand to glide his hard shaft slowly inside her. March winced. But he was behind her and could not see her face. She focused on the memory of that night, willed her body to hunger for him, to accept his physical dominance. He was her husband now and she must be prepared to serve him in all ways.

He said nothing as he gripped her hips with his rough hands and thrust in and out. Gradually, her channel became slick and his drives brought some pleasure. She arched her back and clung tight to her memory. In her mind, she could smell the wood and the metallic scent of his sweat. She could feel the quivering need and hot rush of her blood. Oh, to want. It was the wanting, the chase, she realised now, that had held the meaning for her and Henry. He was the fox, she the prey. And now that the chase had ended, the heart-pounding rush was also gone.

He moved faster and drove in deeper. She gripped the sheets. Soon, he moaned, the sound the same as it had been the night before. Much as he had the night before, he collapsed upon her, saying nothing.

It was not the same, there was no fevered rush that stole her breath and made her insides shatter. But she did not mind. Neither did she mind that the word 'love' was never spoken. It hadn't been spoken between her and Banford, either, she now realised.

Though she belonged to him, though she lived in his shadow, as if she could not be away from him, she was not happy. She did not want to leave him, and yet she did not feel free with him. Everything round her seemed to watch her, seemed to press on her. He had won her, he had her with him, she was his wife. And she—she belonged to him, she knew it. But she was not glad. And he was still foiled. He realised that though he was married to her and possessed her in every possible way, apparently, and though she *wanted* him to possess her, she wanted it, she wanted nothing else, now—still he did not quite succeed.

Something was missing. Instead of her soul swaying with new life, it seemed to droop, to bleed, as if it were wounded. She would sit for a long time with her hand in his, looking away at the sea. And in her dark, vacant eyes was a sort of wound, and her face looked a little peaked. If he spoke to her, she would turn to him with a faint new smile, the strange, quivering little smile of a woman who has died in the old way of love, and can't quite rise to the new way.

She still felt she ought to *do* something, to strain herself in some direction. And there was nothing to do, and no direction in which to strain herself. And she could not quite accept the submergence which his new love put upon her. If she was in love, she ought to *exert* herself, in some way, loving. She felt the weary need of our day to exert herself in love. But she knew that in fact she must no more exert herself in love.

He would not have the love which exerted itself towards him. It made his brow go black. No, he wouldn't let her exert her love towards him. No, she had to be passive, to acquiesce, and to be submerged under the surface of love. She had to be like the seaweeds she saw as she peered down from the boat, swaying forever delicately under water, with all their delicate fibrils put tenderly out upon the flood, sensitive, utterly sensitive and receptive within the shadowy sea, and never, never rising and looking forth above water while they lived. Never. Never looking forth from the water until they died, only then washing, corpses, upon the surface. But while they lived, always submerged, always beneath the wave. Beneath the wave they might have powerful roots, stronger than iron — they might be tenacious and dangerous in their soft waving within the flood. Beneath the water they might be stronger, more indestructible than resistant oak trees are on land. But it was always underwater, always underwater. And she, being a woman, must be like that.

And she had been so used to the very opposite. She had had to take all the thought for love and for life, and all the responsibility. Day after day she had been responsible for the coming day, for the coming year, for her dear Jill's health and happiness and well-being. Verily, in her own small way, she had felt herself responsible for the well-being of the world. And this had been her great stimulant, this grand feeling that, in her own small sphere, she was responsible for the well-being of the world.

And she had failed. She knew that, even in her small way, she had failed. She had failed to satisfy her own feeling of responsibility. It was so difficult. It seemed so grand and easy at first. And the more you tried, the more difficult it became. It had seemed so easy to make one beloved creature happy. And the more you tried, the worse the failure. It was terrible. She had been all her life reaching, reaching, and what she reached for seemed so near, until she had stretched to her utmost limit. Then it was always beyond her.

Always beyond her, vaguely, unrealisably beyond her, and she was left with nothingness at last. The life she reached for, the happiness she reached for, the well-being she reached for all slipped back, became unreal, the farther she stretched her hand. She wanted some goal, some finality — and there was none. Always this ghastly reaching, reaching, striving for something that might be just beyond. Even to make Jill happy. She was glad Jill was dead. For she had realised that she could never make her happy. Jill would always be fretting herself thinner and thinner, weaker and weaker. Her pains grew worse instead of less. It would be so forever. She was glad she was dead.

And if Jill had married a man it would have been just the same. The woman striving, striving to make the man happy, striving within her own limits for the well-being of her world. And always achieving failure. Little, foolish successes in money or in ambition. But at the very point where she most wanted success, in the anguished effort to make some one beloved human being happy and perfect, there the failure was almost catastrophic. You wanted to make your beloved happy, and his happiness seemed always achievable. If only you did just this, that, and the other. And you did this, that, and the other, in all good faith, and every time the failure became a little more ghastly. You could love yourself to ribbons and strive and strain yourself to the bone, and things would go from bad to worse, bad to worse, as far as happiness went. The awful mistake of happiness.

Poor March, in her goodwill and her responsibility, she had strained herself till it seemed to her that the whole of life and everything was only a horrible abyss of nothingness. The more you reached after the fatal flower of happiness, which trembles so blue and lovely in a crevice just beyond your grasp, the more fearfully you became aware of the ghastly and awful gulf of the precipice below you, into which you will inevitably plunge, as into the bottomless pit, if you reach any farther. You pluck flower after flower — it is never *the* flower. The flower itself — its calyx is a horrible gulf, it is the bottomless pit.

That is the whole history of the search for happiness, whether it be your own or somebody else's that you want to win. It ends, and it always ends, in the ghastly sense of the bottomless nothingness into which you will inevitably fall if you strain any farther.

And women — what goal can any woman conceive, except happiness? Just happiness for herself and the whole world. That, and nothing else. And so, she assumes the responsibility and sets off towards her goal. She can see it there, at the foot of the rainbow. Or she can see it a little way beyond, in the blue distance. Not far, not far.

But the end of the rainbow is a bottomless gulf down which you can fall forever without arriving, and the blue distance is a void pit which can swallow you and all your efforts into its emptiness, and still be no emptier. You and all your efforts. So, the illusion of attainable happiness!

Poor March, she had set off so wonderfully towards the blue goal. And the farther and farther she had gone, the more fearful had become the realisation of emptiness. An agony, an insanity at last.

She was glad it was over. She was glad to sit on the shore and look westwards over the sea, and know the great strain had ended. She would never strain for love and happiness any more. And Jill was safely dead. Poor Jill, poor Jill. It must be sweet to be dead.

For her own part, death was not her destiny. She would have to leave her destiny to the boy. But then, the boy. He wanted more than that. He wanted her to give herself without defences, to sink and become submerged in him. And she—she wanted to sit still, like a woman on the last milestone, and watch. She wanted to see, to know, to understand. She wanted to be alone, with him at her side.

And he! He did not want her to watch anymore, to see anymore, to understand anymore. He wanted to veil her woman's spirit, as Orientals veil the woman's face. He wanted her to commit herself to him, and to put her independent spirit to sleep. He wanted to take away from her all her effort, all that seemed her very *raison d'être*. He wanted to make her submit, yield, blindly pass away out of all her strenuous consciousness. He wanted to take away her consciousness, and make her just his woman. Just his woman.

And she was so tired, so tired, like a child that wants to go to sleep, but which fights against sleep as if sleep were death. She seemed to stretch her eyes wider in the obstinate effort and tension of keeping awake. She *would* keep awake. She *would* know. She *would* consider and judge and decide. She would have the reins of her own life between her own hands. She *would* be an independent woman to the last. But she was so tired, so tired of everything. And sleep seemed near. And there was such rest in the boy.

Yet there, sitting in a niche of the high, wild, cliffs of West Cornwall, looking over the westward sea, she stretched her eyes wider and wider. Away to the West, Canada, America. She *would* know and she *would* see what was ahead. And the boy, sitting beside her, staring down at the gulls, had a cloud between his brows and the strain of discontent in his eyes. He wanted her asleep, at peace in him. He wanted her at peace, asleep in him. And there she was, dying with the strain of her own wakefulness. Yet she would not sleep, no, never. Sometimes he thought bitterly that he ought to have left her. He ought never to have killed Banford. He should have left Banford and March to kill one another.

But that was only impatience, and he knew it. He was waiting, waiting to go West. He was aching almost in torment to leave England, to go West, to take March away. To leave this shore! He believed that as they crossed the seas, as they left this England which he so hated, because in some way it seemed to have stung him with poison, she would go to sleep. She would close her eyes at last and give in to him.

Then he would have her, and he would have his own life at last. He chafed, feeling he hadn't got his own life. He would never have it till she yielded and slept in him. Then he would have all his own life as a young man and a male, and she would have all her own life as a woman and a female. There would be no more of this awful straining. She would not be a man anymore, an independent woman with a man's responsibility. Nay, even the responsibility for her own soul she would have to commit to him. He knew it was so, and obstinately held out against her, waiting for the surrender.

"You'll feel better when once we get over the seas to Canada over there," he said to her as they sat among the rocks on the cliff.

She looked away to the sea's horizon, as if it were not real. Then she looked round at him, with the strained, strange look of a child that is struggling against sleep.

"Shall I?" she said.

"Yes," he answered quietly.

And her eyelids dropped with the slow motion, sleep weighing them unconscious. But she pulled them open again to say, "Yes, I may. I can't tell. I can't tell what it will be like over there."

"If only we could go soon!" he said, with pain in his voice.

About the Authors

D.H. Lawrence

David Herbert Lawrence (11 September 1885 – 2 March 1930) was an English novelist, poet, playwright, essayist, literary critic and painter who published as **D.H. Lawrence**. His collected works represent an extended reflection upon the dehumanising effects of modernity and industrialisation. In them, Lawrence confronts issues relating to emotional health and vitality, spontaneity, and instinct.

Isabelle Drake

Thrill-seeking risk takers, heroes with the dark past, sexy locales, untamed women! Isabelle Drake writes stories featuring men and women who aren't afraid to go after what they want. An avid traveller, she'll go just about anywhere—at least once—to meet people and get story ideas.

Isabelle Drake loves to hear from readers. You can find her contact information, website details and author profile page at http://www.total-e-bound.com.

Total-E-Bound Publishing

www.total-e-bound.com

Take a look at our exciting range of literagasmic™
erotic romance titles and discover pure quality
at Total-E-Bound.